STORIES FROM
THE AGE OF DISTRACTION
Volume One: The Island

PRAISE FOR THE ISLAND

"A compelling and pacy journey through the world of storytelling. Along the way it also raises some important questions about the future of humanity in the increasingly fragmented and confusing digital landscape."

Richard Hamilton, The BBC
Author: *The Last Storytellers: Tales from the Heart of Morocco*; *The House of Stories* series

"It is apparent from the moment you open this book that Patricia Mahon not only has a love of words and stories, but also has a great command of our language. In a beautifully written story, Mahon highlights the distraction epidemic that we are all victims to, and alerts us to the need to get back to having face-to-face conversations and storytelling. This small novella offers a large message—positive transformation occurs when we lift our heads up from our devices, engage in the world around us, and reignite our imaginations."

Ellen G. Goldman, M.Ed., Professional Wellness Coach, Writer, Lecturer

"What a fantastic read! Totally un-putdownable. That's not a real word, but should be. I loved the characters, the concept, and the brilliant story. I want to go to all the places mentioned, meet the characters, and if that app truly exists, I want to download it!"

Gina Yashere, International Stand-Up Comedienne and TV Personality

"A wonderful tale that reminds a digital world that, outside of the Internet and away from modern devices, a world full of imagination and adventure still exists. This is a story that reminds readers stories continue to thrive, and imaginations can't be watered down by the advances of modern technology. And that's a good thing."

Mark Esguerra, Marke's World, Travel Photographer, Blogger

"I loved *The Island*!! Very original story, actual, creative and fast-paced, can't put it down once you start. Amazing how it all ends up here at Ilha do Mel. What inspired you? And believe it, there's a woman that comes to my place called Arianna that likes spiritual things! Your description of Ilha do Mel is amazing for someone that's never been here. When you visit us, I will take you 'in loco' to visit the places you described so well. We also have sessions of storytelling practically every day. You see, cell phones don't work properly on the island, which obliges people to actually speak to each other. As a result, people here are very communicative."

Charles Principe, Proprietor of [the real] Pousada Ilha Do Mel, Brazil

"Patricia M. Mahon's contemporary literary fiction work, *Stories from the Age of Distraction: The Island*, is the stuff of dreams. Her heroes, Morgan and Percy, set out to reclaim oral traditions by venturing into the digital domain. Their quest is an ambitious one, and the only open door is through a former roommate of her brother. I had a marvelous time following these otherworldly dreamers as they reach out into the ether and find kindred spirits -- hundreds of them. The stories that evolve are marvelous and work perfectly with the continuing saga of Morgan and Percy.

This work within a work is beautifully scripted with characters who quickly seem like friends and whose quest becomes a universal one. *The Island* is edgy, original and very compelling. It's most highly recommended."
Goodreads Review

"Patricia M. Mahon has done a brilliant job with a topic that has created constant debate . . . with the age of 'virtual society,' people have been losing connection with their loved ones. *Stories from the Age of Distraction: The Island* not only raises voice about the topic, but she actually gives us a solution to the distractions of our age. I really enjoyed that, especially the linguistic abilities of the writer. She made me fall in love with words once again. A really good novel."
Goodreads Review

"I found *Stories from the Age of Distraction: The Island* to be a philosophical read, one in which you really have to step back and admire the overall message, rather than simply the plot itself, which paints a very specific picture of our times and makes an interesting commentary on the future of literature. Overall, I'd recommend this book to readers who enjoy thought-provoking philosophical ideas and educated, revolutionary characters."
Goodreads Review

STORIES FROM THE AGE OF DISTRACTION SERIES
Volume One: The Island

Copyright © 2016 Patricia Mahon

Hardcover ISBN 978-1-939454-65-2
Softcover ISBN 978-1-939454-67-6
Ebook   ISBN 978-1-939454-70-6
Library of Congress Control Number: 2016932755

Cataloging in Publication data pending.

Published in the United States by
Balcony 7 Media and Publishing
530 South Lake Avenue #434
Pasadena, CA 91101
www.balcony7.com

Edited by JZ Bingham www.balcony7.com
Cover & Interior Design by 3 Dog Design www.3dogdesign.com

Trademark attributions of brands/products mentioned in this story are located in the bibliography at the back of this book.

Printed in the United States of America

Distributed to the trade by
Ingram Publisher Services
Mackin
Overdrive
Baker & Taylor (through IPS)
MyiLibrary

STORIES FROM

THE AGE OF DISTRACTION

VOLUME ONE

THE
ISLAND

PATRICIA MAHON

Loving thanks to my mother, Margaret, who taught me the wisdom of respecting input from everyone.

And to my father, Richard, who taught me the gratification of telling those who don't like my work to "go to hell."

PROLOGUE

Stories are the familiar shoes we wear on our long walks through common experience. Since the beginning of time, storytellers have helped to catalog and preserve the human condition. They have held the power of memory, familiarity, and wistfulness over our collective consciousness. The storyteller describes, imparts, paints, and portrays the world with the precision of a timeless artisan. Stories are the verbal albums that chronicle our fleeting days and nights, and the lives of those who came before us. They are the wisdom of mothers, the sage advice of fathers, the admonitions of grandparents, and the easy laughter of a friend.

When life slows down, when our mind seeks sleep, and when our eyes search for dreams . . . it is stories that recline in the back of our mind to ease us into peace.

CHAPTER ONE

Morgan Byrnes, a pale and petite woman of around thirty-five years old, sits in her familiar place in the spare bedroom that has become her office. At her keyboard, her life is completely her own. There's a cup of coffee a fingertip away from her optical mouse that she slides across her Matisse *Studio Under the Eaves* mouse pad. Her diplomas are carefully framed on a long wall with a copy of *My Creed* by Dean Alfange, which hung in her father's office throughout her childhood. She particularly loves this part:

It is my right to be uncommon—if I can. I seek opportunity—not security. I do not wish to be a kept citizen, humbled and dulled by having the state look after me. I want to take the calculated risk; to dream and to build, to fail and to succeed.

Ironically, her father sold insurance. Her mother was an author and Morgan became very familiar with the *tap, tap, tap* of the old IBM typewriter hitting the onion skin during those long summer nights in New Jersey. Each year they went to the shore, and her mother would write about Ireland, or about her stint in a convent, or about lost love. Morgan remembered one scene vividly. . .the description of the Irish church pews in a place called The Village of the Monks:

They were a soft, yellowed wood . . . buffed by tired hands, and polished by the genuflection and soft confessions of impoverished generations seeking Sunday salvation.

1

She was convinced that her mother had a deep, abiding secret that she was either too proper or too genteel to reveal.

Morgan was the first of the personal-word-processor generation. Her Smith Corona™ had a digital screen where she could compose and view an entire sentence at one time, and then hit a button to automatically print it on the page. This was among the first of many new and exciting contraptions that would occupy her life. It had word correction, a dictionary, and a thesaurus built right in. Throughout those cotton-blanket nights at the shore, her *beep, beep, beep* played in chorus to her mother's *tap, tap, tap* late into the evening. No more awkward dabs of Wite-Out®—or the interminable dry-time of Liquid Paper®! Her new single-button Word Erase feature was as free as she had ever been.

In her current office, Morgan is armed with a better keyboard and all the advantages of instant information. She's a corporate speechwriter who makes CEOs and executives sound intelligent and engaged. She's still waiting for her big break—or a stroke of good luck, or a sudden change in fortune.

Beside her desk is the last manuscript her mom handed to her before falling ill and passing on. Morgan has yet to read it, knowing it's a long good-bye. She'll read it someday, just not today.

Like her mother, Morgan tells stories in her spare time. She believes that storytelling is the purest form of human communication. Before there were writing instruments, there were stories. Before there were printers, there were stories. Before IBM and Smith Corona, there were stories. And long before a single transmission was issued by the first packet-switching network—destined to become the Internet—there were stories.

This particular morning, Morgan visits her Facebook page and begins composing on her multimedia Microsoft® Comfort

Keyboard 5000. She taps out a series of lines, then a responding post appears.

Morgan smiles and reads aloud:

She was isolated, alone in a digital world without human contact, except for her companion . . .

She sits back and watches as the rest of the reply from Percy Chadwick—her best friend and business partner—slowly crawls across her screen.

Felix, her cat, who is actually a lynx. She has other exotic pets, as well as her favorite, Casey . . .

Morgan writes:

. . . a camel that she rescued from a wildlife reserve in Chad, where he had been recovering from an accident at the hands of a careless British vacationer . . .

Percy replies:

. . . who struck Casey while behind the wheel of his black Range Rover. Simon, who should never have been driving, had been drinking a local brew called . . .

Morgan tacks on:

. . . Chad Travail Ale, an ancient malt with a hint of ginger and overtones of rich clove. It is said you can never have just one.

A new name appears in the writing exchange. Frank Turner adds:

But he'd had far more than that, nestled in the corner of the Kakaki Lounge where the Travail Ale flowed freely. Simon was in Chad to coach football, his first love. His second was ale.

Another new name chimes in. Jennifer Mays offers a line:

Gwyneth, his wife, had always thought that she was the light in Simon's eyes, but he had stopped looking at her years ago, and she slowly took her place behind men and football pitches, dark bars, and endless glasses of ale.

Morgan sits back in her chair in disbelief, as more people from all over the world add lines to the story.

Dylan Donnelly types:

Simon's best friend, Nigel, was traveling with the couple. He was not a footballer but an endangered-wildlife photographer in search of the African wild dog. He spent long nights at the edge of camp, trying to capture the nocturnal movements of the mottled, long-legged, bat-eared canine, whose dwindling numbers are scattered across the sub-Saharan regions of East Africa.

Steven Wyatt follows with:

Gwyneth sometimes joined Nigel by the fire, long after Simon had raised his glass a dozen times to his team, in a resounding pronouncement of "God Bless the Queen."

Josef Auttenberg continues:

She was beautiful by the fire but, then again—to him—she was perfect in every way. To be alone with her was a quiet form of anguish.

Nina Marquez adds:

When Gwyneth was beside him, Nigel tried to occupy himself with his camera lens, but his hands trembled, and he lost control of his eyes, his lips, and his throat.

Jerome Robinson interjects:

He would cough and bite his lip to disguise the quivering, and dismiss it all as a head cold.

Amelie Belanger joins in:

Low flames glowed in the fireplace at the Kakaki Lounge on the night of the crash. Simon sat at a high table with full pints, courtesy of the football lads. It was a glorious victory and he downed large mouthfuls of single malt to mark the occasion.

Franz Wilhem writes:

Still in his mud-caked cleats and blood-stained jersey, Simon sang crude and whimsical songs, and talked about changing the world.

Joe Nardozzi offers:

But like the old Knobthorn Lounge sign out front, it was a world he had pissed on. Simon was a blowhard and a ne'er-do-well and when he lumbered out of the bar half-cocked, his buddies just let him go.

Percy adds:

If not the camel, he would have run over something else.

Morgan continues:

Gwyneth tried to go after him, as any dutiful wife would, but Simon raced through the darkness with a wet mouth and wet pants, at drunken, break-neck speed.

Percy adds:

The crash could be heard across the sloping plains and beyond the marsh fields. The camel was bawling in a low squeal, not all that different from Simon's rendition of "Whiskey in the Jar."

Vitale Dibenedetto offers:

A local herder named Zaid said the camel was his and should be put out of its misery. He pulled a rifle from a sack strapped to his back, but when Nigel arrived on the scene, he yelled, "Stop!" and threw himself in front of the camel's broken body.

Nancy Harrington continues:

Gwyneth rushed up behind Nigel, her hands over her mouth. She looked at the camel and then over at Simon, who was swearing and cussing from somewhere in the overturned wreckage of the Range Rover. She ran to the camel.

Morgan sends Percy a private message that pops up on his computer screen: *Who are these people?*

Percy replies: *I have no idea. Friends of yours? Friends of mine?*

Morgan writes back, shaking her head: *I don't know a single one of them!*

Dylan Donnelly continues contributing to the quickly evolving story:

Gwyneth paid Zaid a handsome sum and made arrangements to take the camel to a prominent veterinarian in N'Djamena. Simon left Chad and made his own arrangements with a waitress back at the Dew Drop Inn in Oxford.

Percy adds:

All the rugby boys knew Tilly, and Tilly knew them.

Alfred Klemmer states:

Afterward Nigel helped Gwyneth transport Casey back to the United Kingdom, where he recuperated on her lush farm in Birmingham.

Jennifer Mays interjects:

Despite remaining married to Simon, Gwyneth never heard from him again. She would receive a letter from Nigel every few months. The last one came from Burundi, where he was tracking down a certain type of swamp mouse on the brink of extinction.

Frank Turner writes:

Gwyneth remained alone with her animals on the large piece of property left to her by her father.

Morgan concludes:

She named the camel "Casey" after an Irishman she had met on a street corner in New York on Saint Patrick's Day. His last name was Meaney, but it turns out he wasn't mean at all.

Morgan leans back, grabs her cell phone, and frantically taps out a text to Percy: *Meet me at the coffee shop right away!*

He reads it and types back: *Said Gwyneth, who now spends her days drinking anise-flavored liquor and reciting endless lines of Tennyson.*

Morgan rolls her eyes and fires back: *No, Percy…in real time! Not story time. Meet me now, please!*

Morgan signs out of Facebook and shuts down her computer. She feverishly writes on a notepad and then looks around her room, strewn with folders, papers, and overflowing shelves of books. On one wall are the Irish authors: Yeats, Shaw, Synge, and O'Casey. On the other wall are the English poets: Milton, Blake, Byron, and Coleridge.

Morgan stares at her desk and then slaps the table. "That's it! That is it! How could I not have seen this before? How did everyone else miss this?" She tears off several notebook pages and crams them into a folder and dashes out the door.

———●———

Percy is seated at a table of a local coffee shop, sipping from a white mug. He's forty-something and handsome, with trim blond hair and a lean, tan body. Morgan jumps into a seat across from him.

"Oh my God, Percy!" Morgan says, exasperated.

Percy looks her over and responds without urgency, "You interrupted a perfectly fascinating story. By the way, who are Franz Wilhem and Josef Auttenberg? I checked out their profiles. They both look like cutie-pies!"

"I don't know. I don't know who any of them are. Isn't that incredible! Did you see what happened, Percy?"

"A bunch of people are suddenly stalking you on Facebook?"

Morgan rolls her eyes again. "No. They came for the story. Do you get that? And they came from all over the world."

"It's a good story, Morgan. I have to hand it to us. We took it from California's Central Valley to Central Africa in mere seconds."

"It's not our story, Percy. It belongs to everyone who joined in."

"Everybody certainly brought something," Percy smiles. "I'm not too sure about that swamp-mouse research but, to each his own."

"The story made its way to a dark ale house on another continent. I could see it, couldn't you? I could smell the old wooden chairs and the bar top. I could taste the foam on the ale!" exclaims Morgan.

Percy nods and replies, "It was like an old movie from back in the days when they really went to those places in order to film them."

"People love to tell stories, Percy. They're hungry for it—ravenous actually. The digital age is an imagination killer. We've lost the ability to describe, portray, or say anything. We think in acronyms. We truncate. We're losing our oral tradition!" she declares.

Percy sips his coffee, looks across at Morgan, and then around the café, which is scattered with people on cell phones and laptops. "Yeah . . . and?" he replies.

She tosses her notes on the table. "Do you understand that we'll be the first generation who fails to tell our collective narrative? We're on the verge of losing our identity. We'll be extinct to the ages."

Percy doesn't respond. He stares down at the table as Morgan glances around the coffee shop, shaking her head. She's in one of her passionate rants, so he knows better than to say anything. They've been friends for over a decade and when she's in a heated harangue he just lets her work through it.

Without thinking, he picks up his cell phone but quickly puts it down again, realizing it's not a good time to play on his handheld. All around the room, no one is engaged with the world or with each other. The café is an array of slouching shoulders and dangling headsets, huddled in a cocoon of self, silently interacting with their chosen gadget. One woman brushes her finger along a tablet and another presses on her cell phone while two men in the corner each tap on portable keyboards.

"From the Bible to the Ancient Greeks, from the Early Chinese to the Native Americans, every civilization had a collection of stories that captured and held the human experience for generations. *The Legends of King Arthur,* the *Arabian Knights, Aesop's Fables, The Iliad* and the *Odyssey, The Canterbury Tales, Sleeping Beauty, The Ugly Duckling* . . ." she continues.

"Perhaps stories are like fruitcakes. Only a few were ever created, but they just keep circulating," Percy says with a smirk.

"Some stories have survived almost thirty thousand years, long before there was a printing press, or a word processor, or an Internet," Morgan tells him.

"What on earth did they do thirty thousand years ago?" he asks.

"They talked. They sang. They recited. And they performed," she offers.

"You would think technology would make communication easier."

"That's the irony, Percy. It's shut everything down! A few years ago this place was humming with poets, storytellers, and performance artists. Look at it now," she says in a low voice.

"They just can't help themselves, Morgan. They like the instant gratification," he replies.

"We used to sing this song in my Catholic grammar school called 'He's Got the Whole World in His Hands,' referring to God, of course," she says. "Who knew that one day the whole world would literally be in our hand, on a handheld device? Think about the madness of a contraption that's replaced the phone, the TV, the radio, the Dewey decimal system, and meaningful conversation."

"They'll never give up their phones," he whispers.

"I'm not asking them to give them up. I just want them to connect—not disconnect—and to tell a collective story much like we did this morning," she replies.

"The question is, Morgan . . . can they? Technology has brought a degree of detachment and preoccupation that makes the boob tube look downright cerebral," he adds.

"They can. They just need to be taught how," she says.

"But we've become so linguistically hollow," he laments.

"Everybody likes stories, Percy. They're a uniquely human thing and always have been, from cave paintings to oral lore—to books, to radio, to film, to TV, to the Internet!" she states with passion.

"And how shall you teach them, when their faces are always in their phones?" he asks.

"I'm going to create an app!" she exclaims.

"For Facebook?" he asks, bemused.

"An app that lets anyone, at any time, from any place in the world, add to a global narrative and tell a collective story," she explains.

"You want to develop an app?" he repeats, his brows rising.

"I want to create a communication renaissance," she clarifies.

"Morgan, dear heart, you're the third person I've met this month who has an idea for an app," he says.

"I'm not talking about an easier way to book a restaurant or to find a hotel. I'm talking about creating a shared, interactive, global story in an effort to save our generation's narrative," she tells him, point blank.

Percy looks at her carefully and realizes that she's quite serious. His role in their relationship ranges from naysayer, to pragmatist, to champion. He must handle this judiciously. Morgan has many worthy ambitions and more grand thoughts on a Tuesday afternoon than some can muster in a lifetime. He's always thought that if any single one of them "hits," he could say *he knew her when*.

"It sounds brilliant on so many levels, but expensive," he murmurs.

"Forget the money for a second . . . What do you think about the concept? You're one of the most intelligent men I know," she adds.

"Flattery will get you everywhere. What do I think? I think it's downright genius. We're in piss-poor shape as a civilization. We Google around in character-limited cyber prisons. We write in a new fast-thumbed alphabet that has shortchanged meaning. We've replaced emotions with acronyms. We've lost our sense of satire. We've abbreviated away our imaginations. We're an electronic shadow of our former storytelling selves!" he states in a rare eruption of emotion.

"Will you help me, Percy?" she asks.

"I teach part-time and I dream full-time. Alas, I have no money, Morgan," he replies.

"I will find the money. I just need you," she says with determination.

She looks into his eyes. He looks around the coffeehouse and takes in the peculiar quiet of the dropped heads of the real-time generation; swiping through vacation photos, mundane milestones, political shares, and pet videos of their virtual friends. Only the sound of the occasional ring tone, the errant spoon on a plate, and the blast of the espresso maker shatters a perfectly sad commentary on human interaction.

He smiles and announces, "I shall be your champion!"

She leans across the table and gently kisses his cheek. "Just be my friend, Percy," she whispers.

CHAPTER TWO

Morgan is back at her desk, frantically drafting lists of potential investors. Each time she gets fatigued, she looks across the room at the framed authors and poets on her wall. They've been with her through high school, college, studies abroad, and graduate school. They've peered at her from the cold walls of her Dublin dorm, a fireplace mantel in a grand living room of the Deep South, and the hot walls of her pink casita in the dry Sonoran Desert.

"I bet you never thought that storytelling would teeter on the verge of extinction, gentlemen. Then again, I bet you never thought a woman in the twenty-first century would try to save it by creating a special page in an electronic book that allows all the world to speak at once, out of thin air," she mutters.

She goes to Google and researches "app development costs," and her screen fills with banner ads, app cost estimators, development reviews, and infographs. App development seems to be quite the business, replete with its share of warnings, horror stories, offshore nightmares, and rip-off reports.

"We build apps for $25 an hour!" she reads aloud. "Sounds too good to be true because it clearly is," she exclaims. She reads further and then sits back in her chair in astonishment. Where would she get $100,000?

At that moment she realizes that her literary heroes were not rich men. They were often underprivileged observers, slogging in urban decay or rural impoverishment, with so few possessions that their only means of survival was to build a better place in their minds. The titans of the tall tale, the giants of folklore, the masters of narrative, the wizards of words, and the timeless storytellers who preserved our human vernacular were often societal indigents.

"A lack of money did not stop Blake. Rural hardship did not impede Synge," she states aloud. "And it won't stop me. My app will be different. When the app companies hear my concept, they'll just *want* to develop it!"

Morgan takes a deep breath and dials the first number on her list. She encounters both working numbers and nonworking, and a variety of call centers with distinctly offshore accents from developers presumably in Manila, Mumbai, Moscow, and Ho Chi Minh City. When she finally reaches some stateside companies, they're unmoved by her concept and indifferent about the work. They ask about budgets and functionality. They inquire about mobile strategies, platforms, and data sources. They query her about content, updates, and user experience, and claim a turnaround of up to a year.

Suddenly, she's a very small fish in a large cyberpond, teeming with oodles of wide-eyed, T-shirted digital savants with robust app concepts designed to promote mindlessness and distraction. She needs to do this the old-fashioned way, by pounding the pavement. She sets up some reluctant appointments, uses MapQuest to nail down her routes, engages Percy as her copilot, and loads up the car for an adventure to the world's foremost high-tech mecca, just south of San Francisco Bay.

The hundreds of miles of coastline that separate Los Angeles and Silicon Valley are anything but virtual. It's rugged, raw, natural, and in many respects, the vision of a lifetime as the coast rolls, falls, and collapses into the sea. Names like Morro Bay, Cambria, San Simeon, Big Sur, and Bixby Creek Bridge evoke images of wild shorelines, tumbling vistas, and inspired panoramas where the land and water greet each other in a recurring cycle of passionate whispers.

There's something cathartic and liberating about the highway. America's long gray roads hold her lifeblood. The pulse of passing cars slowly dissipates into the tangled turns and blind corners of life on the move. The open road was how people kept in touch for generations.

Morgan thinks about the time before cell phones, when a long journey meant a long silence, and an even longer good-bye. How did we do it? Before her grown-up life, she would drive for hours on the weekends to see her friends at the Jersey Shore— navigating the turnpike from Woodcliff Lake, Elmwood Park, Clifton, Bloomfield, and East Orange. Everyone assumed she would get there. If she didn't . . . surely they would find out. Or would they? Those were the days of bodysurfing and beer, of boardwalks and sugar bees, of hot dogs and Parcheesi. Sitting on hot towels, slathered in QT and Coppertone® . . . she and her friends, were masters of the beach.

She would return home a little more tired and a lot more sunburned. Who could forget those stutter stops along the Garden State Parkway, and the quarter tosses into the white toll baskets as she pulled her sunburned back off the car seat. By Exit 128, the summer was a distant memory. She would gas up and wait in line for the pay phone. *The pay phone!* Through the hundred miles of parkway, she'd never felt afraid. Was it safer back then, simply because people looked at one another? Was it safer because we said *Hello*?

Percy continues to drive as Morgan thinks about her app. She looks across at his hands loosely clasping the wheel. He has *freeway freeze*, that mesmerized state where a driver's mind slips in and out like the struts between the guardrail and the shoulder of the road. *What a good friend.* She can tell him anything without the risk of being judged. She can tell him about the melancholy and the angst, about the dark shadows and the madcap dreams. Was she dragging him on another fool's errand? She turns back to the road just in time to catch the magnificence of the sun as it slowly tucks in behind a glorious crimson curtain of evening.

"Pink sky at night, sailor's delight," she announces.

"Will there be sailors tomorrow?" Percy asks with a wink.

"It means fair weather, Percy. It was an old maritime method of predicting the elements, long before satellites and voice navigation," she says.

"Remember gas station maps?" he jokes.

"Absolutely! It was a rite of passage the first time you could fold one," she replies.

"Remember magnetic checkers?" he asks.

"Of course—my stocking stuffers all through college. We never really played with them."

"Remember not having a cup holder in the car?" he chuckles.

"How about pre-Starbucks™! How did we stay awake?" she wonders.

"Or bottled water. What did we drink?" he adds.

"Or satellite radio. What did we listen to?" she laughs.

"Bob Segar. We listened to Bob Segar," he replies.

"Springsteen, Percy. Everyone listened to Springsteen," she tells him.

"Do we sound like our parents? Did they go on about Sinatra and Sammy Davis, Jr., like this?" he muses.

"Mine went on about Perry Como and Petula Clark," she adds.

"Petula Clark! I haven't thought about her in years. I always loved her name . . . Petula," he exclaims.

Morgan starts to sing, "When you're alone, and life is making you lonely, you can always go . . . downtown."

"Wow, Morgan. What part of your mind did you pull that from?" he asks.

"The part where my father's eight-track is sitting on the floor of our sunroom. The part where he's still alive on a Sunday afternoon, stirring a rum and Coke™, and watching *Meet the Press* in his madras Bermuda shorts," she answers.

"Amazing."

"What?" she replies.

"How do you remember things so clearly?"

"Are you kidding? I have complete houses in my mind, with my parents and grandparents in them. I have bright and vivid rooms in my head. I have green lawns and very specific trees. I have pumpkin patches and schoolrooms. I could tell you where I sat in the third grade and who sat next to me on either side," she answers.

"That's a lot to hold."

"It's very tiring. Everything is in there clamoring to get out and walk around," she admits.

"No matter what happens, Morgan, I wouldn't trade this time in the car with you for anything," he tells her with a smile.

"Thank you, Percy. You *get* me," she smiles back.

"I do. Lord help me, but I do get you," he replies.

"So tomorrow we start operation World Wide Writes!" she exclaims.

"Great name. Is that what you're calling it?" he asks.

"Yes, and *writes* is spelled w-r-i-t-e-s. Do you like it?"

"Very clever."

"Ladies and Gentlemen," Morgan shouts, in a mock announcer's voice. "This is an app that will change the world!"

"I'm sure they've never heard that before," he says with a smirk.

"This is *go big or go home*, right? These Silicons are leap-of-faith people, are they not?" she asks.

"Supposedly, but they're also arrogant and jaded profiteers who are about as traditional as a selfie," he conveys. "I may be wrong, Morgan, but I don't think saving the human vernacular is going to be high on their bucket list. They make their livelihood keeping people distracted."

"We just have to convince them that they can make a difference and make money at the same time," she replies.

"I understand, but if they have bad clothes, bad manners, and bad breath, I'll have to excuse myself. Who are we meeting first?" he asks.

"The first two are, more or less, cold calls."

"More or less?" he presses.

"Okay, more than less. They're unsolicited," she admits.

"Morgan, we're going to get thrown out on our old-school asses," he exclaims.

"We just have to play the game, Percy. Remember, Silicon Valley isn't a place. It's a state of mind. We just need to act like we belong here," she tells him.

"I see," he replies. "Okay, I can do that."

"I'm going to talk about smart phones, smart wind, and smart TV," she states.

"And I just read an article about green coffins made from bamboo and wicker," he shares.

"Perfect! See. You can do it," she exclaims.

"I'm doing this for you, Morgan. The thought of striking up a conversation with people who carry solar backpacks is more than I can bear."

"It'll be worth our while, Percy. Our third meeting was set up by my brother, with a guy he went to school with, who has an app development firm."

"Well, bust my buttons! Why didn't you say that in the first place? That's a horse of a different color," he says with relief.

They continue to drive along stretches of now-sparse, gray highway. It gets less picturesque as the coastline leaves them. They roll across farmland and the scorched earth of what's been a long, hot California summer. There's nothing as far as the eye can see, except road, sunburned hills, an occasional cluster of cows, and the blinding glare of the setting sun.

"Los Gatos," he says, looking at a *Welcome* sign out the window. "The cats?"

"Must be named after the mountain lions," she replies.

"Wonderful. Remind me not to carry around raw meat while I'm here," he counters.

"It was their turf long before we came," she tells him while glancing out the window at the densely wooded foothills.

"I'm not going to argue with them," he says.

Morgan and Percy roll into the relatively quiet town just on the perimeter of Silicon Valley. It's a charming, small village with pristine Victorian-era homes and commercial buildings. The historic architecture houses boutiques, coffeehouses, wine-tasting rooms, pubs, salons, and dessert shops.

"This is where they all come to play, Percy."

"Who?" he asks.

"The Silicons," she answers. Morgan suddenly points. "And that is where we're staying!"

Percy hits the brakes and pulls into the driveway of the Best Western hotel. "The *Inn of Los Gatos*," he mutters.

"It was under $200 a night," she asserts.

"Hey, no arguments here. Big day tomorrow. Just get me to my crib," he says.

After a brief check-in, bag-lugging, and the rap and hum of a noisy elevator, the pair wheel wearily down the hall to retire in adjoining rooms. Morgan's standard room has the smell of travel, clinched inside the faux wood plantation shutters. The carpet has those odd, circular, spherical, and spatial patterns of brown, orange, and maroon that can only be found in late-night lodges and brief, forgettable stopovers. The walls are a roadhouse gallery of wine art, hotel still-lifes, and framed prints of perky cats perched on fabric chairs. They're domesticated and cute, not the kind that likely prowled the valley when the town got its name. Everything is nailed to the walls.

She stumbles into the white-on-white bathroom, washes her face with sample soaps, and pulls a toothbrush across her teeth. She looks tired and feels somewhat ridiculous. Her life has been a series of "almosts," "not-quites," and "could-have-beens." She expected her dreams to come true by now, but they've been unruly and unrealized. Each day she struggles with the pull of mediocrity and the easy lure of commonness that her father had rebuked so long ago. She'd watched countless wide eyes droop when facing the naysaying, and the apathy that sets in when one tires of struggling against the tide. Morgan believed she was different.

She could have melded with the masses, folded into the flock, and crowd-surfed her way to an utterly comfortable existence. The road "more traveled," however, was not on her map. She wanted the other path, the one so overgrown, overlooked, and abandoned that the earth had literally taken it back. She knew that if dreams were indeed out there, this must be where they reside. She would need to push through the thicket and scrape through the brush for the sake of the mental pictures, the sensations, the sounds, and the moments in time that only stories can impart.

Morgan tucks herself into bed. She can hear cars in the parking lot and late check-ins on the stairway. She needs to sleep. Tomorrow, she comes face-to-face with all those polished and pandered "Silicons"—the overindulged, overstimulated fingertip generation. They'll look at her as a somewhat silly woman, with a somewhat sillier app idea, before running off to the *Loving Hut* for some royal noodle soup, or the *Coupa Café* for a ginger lemongrass tea, or a quick game of Ping-Pong down the hall.

She'll try to tell them that stories are really what connect us and that every techno-pathway they create is only as good as the message it carries. The narrative has been the single unifying force of human civilization, giving us context and critical meaning. But *"the falcon cannot hear the falconer."* Leave it to Yeats to perfectly describe our monumental disconnect.

When they dismiss her, she must go back in her mind to that frothy pint of Chad Travail Ale and remember the magic of storytelling that propelled her to Room #276 of the *Inn of Los Gatos*.

CHAPTER THREE

As the sun rises over Silicon Valley, one perceives an interesting mix of angles and reflections. Like consummate gray matter, countless steely communal structures align within lobes of water and trees folded into larger canyons and ridges. It's a solar-panel jungle where finding a building without a logo is about as rare as finding a café without a venture capitalist, a techno-kingpin, or a budding entrepreneur. They're all here. The titans of the virtual connection: Apple, Cisco, Oracle and, of course, Yahoo.

Morgan can't help but play with the names. Who can think of an apple without recalling the temptation of Eve? A cisco is actually a small, white migratory fish. An oracle is a prophet and, in many respects, a storyteller. And Morgan has always associated a yahoo with the rough, filthy and "disagreeable animals" of *Gulliver's Travels*.

Percy and Morgan arrive at their first appointment. The lobby is austere and industrial, the receptionist is young and unfocused. Her desk holds more than one iPhone®, iPad®, and iMac®, as well as a small MacBook Air®. Morgan and Percy watch her black French-manicured nails tap, pull, drag, and swipe along each device—a maestro of the modern switchboard!

"We're here to see Ethan," Morgan announces, leaning over the counter.

"Do you have an appointment?" the young woman asks without looking up.

"We do not, but your website says to '*stop by anytime with new and exciting ideas to develop,*'" she answers.

"What's your idea?" the receptionist inquires while tapping on the iPad.

Morgan looks at Percy and smiles. "It's an app concept," she replies.

"Okay...So, like, they're all in a training meeting right now? So I doubt anyone will be able to see you. If you can just fill this out, I'll send it along," she says, handing Morgan a blank iPad screen.

They arrive at the next technology company. Like the last, this office has a reclaimed factory look—hanging pipes and an open duct system. Years ago, offices were finished with drop ceilings, clean lines, and crown molding, but the new trend is evidently "old industry:" raw beams, metal conduit, and dangling sprinkler heads. With a little paint and some selective shine, these endearing symbols of hole-punching, clock-watching hourly labor have now become recycled chic.

"Hi, we're here to see Aaron, please," Morgan says to a young woman whose head is barely visible above two large computer screens.

The woman looks up briefly to scan Morgan and Percy. "What is this regarding?"

"We wanted to discuss the development of a new app," Morgan responds.

"And what kind is it?" she asks.

"Meaning native, hybrid, or mobile?" Morgan queries.

"No, what does the app do?" the woman retorts.

"Well, it's not really something I want to summarize over a countertop. Suffice it to say, it's very different, and I'd prefer to speak directly to Aaron about it." Morgan says firmly.

The woman stares at her. "Unless I have an idea of what the app does, I can't pass it on."

Percy quickly jumps in. "Sure you can. You're not a developer, and I highly doubt that you have a say in what app concepts the firm takes on. If you don't ask him to give us a few minutes of his time, we're going to get our app developed elsewhere and when it goes live and has thousands of downloads a day, I'm going to send him an email and tell him that we were standing in his lobby with our idea, and you wouldn't so much as pass on a message."

She looks at both of them again and starts typing. "He says he'll give you five minutes…in five minutes," she mutters.

"Fair enough!" Percy states as he and Morgan make their way toward a pair of orange plastic chairs.

"I haven't seen chairs like this since my last colonoscopy," Percy whispers.

Morgan giggles. "Hopefully, we won't be in them very long."

From the unique vantage point only afforded by molded lobby furniture, Morgan and Percy observe troops of young techies come and go from the building. They're in jeans, sweatshirts, and sneakers, all possessing the same look of preoccupation and fixation. They talk about clean code, dirty code, code slush, code freeze, hacking, and password protection as they hit daylight with eye-shielding discomfort.

"Those are the vampires of systems analysis," Percy says.

"It's been more than five minutes," Morgan mumbles.

"I know," Percy responds.

"I think we were played," she replies.

"I think you're right," he agrees.

Morgan stands up and hops atop another armless, plastic orange chair. She clears her throat, lifts her chin, and begins to recite. "The year is 1876, and Western Union is one of the most powerful communications companies in the country, if not the world. Weary and broke from years of challenges to their purported invention of the telephone, Alexander Graham Bell and his financial backer, Gardiner G. Hubbard, approach the communications giant with an offer to sell their patent for the telephone for a mere $100,000. Western Union deploys a team of investigators to review the proposal and ascertain the phone's viability, not only as a communications tool but as an investment.

"The team concludes that sending speech over telegraph wires has a host of shortcomings and is, ultimately, not technically feasible. They go on to state that Bell's and Hubbard's predictions about widespread phone usage are 'fanciful' and 'wild-eyed,' and call the notion of a telephone in every city downright 'idiotic.' Western Union executives ultimately deem the $100,000 request for the sale of the patent to be 'utterly unreasonable,' and tout the superiority of the telegraph by comparison.

"Such is the arrogance of 'moment in time' superiority. The foolhardiness of those who believe they have cornered the market on 'change' fill the 'never-heard-of,' 'little-known' registries of history. Those riding the flavors of the decade often grossly underestimate the world's ability to reinvent itself again and again, and are often too cavalier, cocky, and bombastic to see the Next Great Thing coming."

Her speech completed, Morgan glances across at the receptionist, who's now wearing headphones. Morgan looks down at Percy, who smiles and offers a slow-clap; the solitary applause echos and reverberates through the large, hollow space. She steps down from her orange plastic podium and the pair leave the building, eager for their next appointment.

The third lobby is not all that different from the two before it except when Morgan mentions her name, the woman at the desk smiles. Seeing this as an opening, Morgan adds that her brother went to MIT with one of the principals. This factoid further softens her demeanor.

"Your brother really went to MIT with one of the head guys?" Percy whispers to Morgan.

"Yes," Morgan smiles, "Brad Fielding!"

"I assume you told the latest gatekeeper of the Emerald City?" he asks.

"Of course," she replies. "I also told her that I was Dorothy."

Morgan and Percy are waved into a small glass-walled conference room. The sign outside the door says THE FISHBOWL. They take a seat on two white, vinyl chairs tucked underneath a frosted glass-top table. Despite their visibility, no one seems to be able to see them, which prompts Percy to do his imitation of an angry blowfish.

Beyond the glass walls are scores of people on swivel chairs, ergo stools, yoga balls, and footrests. Employees sit at trendy, long blue and green tables propped in front of computer screens with coffee cups, headsets, and earphones; all arranged in a "people efficient" format that maximizes comfort and productivity.

"*Ahhh.* The Silicons!" Percy says, gesturing at them.

"Up close and personal," Morgan notes.

"So what exactly does Brad Fielding do here at App Storm?"

"He decides what to develop and what not to develop. He could decide to fund our app this afternoon and literally pluck us from obscurity," Morgan states with confidence.

"Fabulous. If I wasn't so hungry, I'd be downright excited."

"Being hungry is good, Percy," she tells him. "Too much food makes you satisfied and complacent."

"So, have you met Brad?" he asks.

"Once, maybe twelve or fifteen years ago at a keg party in my brother's dorm. It was your typical frat gathering of drunk, gel-haired wise-asses," she reminisces.

"What does he look like?"

"Short, average . . . a smirky wise guy in a faded, twilight-plaid J.Crew Indian-cotton shirt, tracking time on his steel Bremont and watching the struggling world through his Moscot readers."

"You forgot 'while restlessly tapping his Testoni suede derby lace-ups,'" Percy states.

"Of course. Good point as always, my friend," she says with a smile.

"Too bad they're all so linear. I wouldn't mind a nice Silicon Valley industrialist to talk techy to me," Percy muses.

"That's only after they talk techy to me first. I have to have this app, Percy! I have my heart set on it," she exclaims.

"Morgan, I would never distract your uber-rich young investor—unless, of course, you ask me to. Do you have your pitch down?" he asks.

"I think so. Do you have the slide show?" Morgan repeatedly glances through the glass wall, looking for anyone moving in their direction. Percy suddenly gasps, pulls out his laptop, and starts it up.

"Okay, PowerPoint® is queued up. Now, let's have the pitch," he commands.

"Right now?" she asks.

"My dear, there's no time like the absolute present. I mean, really. What are we risking here? Over-preparation?"

"You're right," Morgan admits.

She stands up to face Percy.

"Gentlemen, thank you for your time today. I can't tell you how fortunate I feel to be able to meet with you. I appreciate the time that you have set aside out of your busy schedules—"

"I'm bored!" Percy interrupts. "I've heard it all before. Blah, blah, blah. Lady, just get to the pitch."

"I am! I was just trying to be polite," she complains.

"You can't afford to be polite, Morgan. And they don't have the time to listen to your pandering. So spare everyone the niceties and get to the point!" he snaps.

"Fine!" she snaps back.

Morgan composes herself and starts her pitch again.

"I am about to share the greatest breakthrough in human communication since the very first books were printed during China's Tang Dynasty back in 618 . . ." she commands.

"Better! You've got my attention," Percy gushes.

At that moment, three men in khakis and sports shirts whip around the corner, swing open the glass doors, and quickly enter the room. The shortest of the three smiles at Morgan and Percy and extends his hand.

"Brad Fielding, and these are my associates, Chase Wrigley and Mark Hadler," he says.

Morgan stands, grabs his hand, and calmly replies, "Morgan Byrnes, and my business partner, Percy Chadwick. It's good to see you again, Brad."

"Gentlemen, Morgan's brother went to MIT with me. We were actually roommates, so I told Brent that we would have a sit-down with Morgan to discuss her new app concept," he says.

"Certainly. Chase Wrigley," says the tallest of the three as he shakes both Morgan's and Percy's hands.

"Hi, Mark Hadler," says the third man, who appears to be the oldest of the group. "So tell us about your concept."

They all sit down at the table as Morgan straightens up in her chair. "I appreciate the meeting, gentlemen, truly. I know how busy you are and how many app ideas you must see in the course of a week . . ."

"Morgan, we're more than happy to give you our thoughts," states Brad Fielding.

"So what's the app?" asks Hadler.

Percy glances at her with a subtle nod and a smile. Morgan acknowledges him with her eyes and quickly changes her tone from gracious to straightforward.

"The app is called World Wide Writes, as in w-r-i-t-e-s. It's a global forum through which the world writes a collective story by contributing one or two lines at a time, from anywhere in the country, across the continent or around the globe. A story could start in a coffee shop here in Mountain View, go to a backyard barbecue in Kansas City, ride onboard the A train in New York, and end up at a beerhall in Vienna, depending on who contributes . . ."

A brief silence fills the room, soon broken by Hadler.

"Why?" he asks, somewhat slouched in his chair and shrugging his shoulders.

"Rudyard Kipling once said, '*If history were taught in the form of stories, it would never be forgotten,*'" she answers.

Morgan meets Hadler's eyes and draws more confidence. "Let me be more direct. People love to tell stories, and the digital age is robbing us of oral tradition. We've forgotten how to express ourselves with full thoughts and whole words—and if we don't make a change, we'll be the first civilization incapable of conveying its own narrative.

"Gentlemen, mankind has been telling stories for thousands of years. Cave walls were the first blank pages, and stories have been the guardians of human learning. They're how we've come to understand our limitations, as well as our possibilities. They're how we first felt fear and admonition, and how we learned of daring and adventure. Science has finally just confirmed that stories activate different parts of our brain, where we cull deeper meaning and where the words of the storyteller actually mingle with our own experiences."

"We like to say that, here in the twenty-first century, we're actually so connected, we're disconnected," Percy adds.

"How will the app work?" Wrigley asks.

To Morgan, that question implies a degree of interest. She suddenly loses her train of thought and looks down at the table.

Percy jumps in again. "Much like Facebook, Twitter, Pinterest, or any existing platform with a fixed-character field. We'll toss out a story cue, and then anyone from anywhere and at anytime can write the next line."

"And what exactly is a 'story cue'?" asks Fielding.

"Glad you asked," Percy replies. "We actually did screen grabs of one of our recent Facebook stories and loaded it into a PowerPoint. I'd like to show how this particular story evolved, and you can follow along frame by frame. Morgan, can you please read the contributed lines?"

"Absolutely, and at the bottom of each frame, we added the contributor's location, so you can see both the national and international flavor of the storytellers," she replies.

They all gather around Percy's computer as lines appear on the screen. Morgan reads the first slide in a clear and succinct voice.

"Tatiana was certain she had seen this place before. It looked and felt familiar." Morgan waits for the next slide.

"There was something about the tablecloths and the dangling lights, dingy with old talk and cigarettes." She pauses, watching the screen for her next cue.

"She knew the three men huddled in the corner, the blond-haired woman at the bar, and the handsome bartender."

"She even knew the old man at the piano, who played a tune that made her at once sad and anxious."

"So have you tested this?" Hadler blurts out impulsively.

"We did. It was infectious," Morgan replies.

"So what did they write next? Keep going." Fielding prompts.

Percy reads now, while advancing each frame. *"It was summertime, long ago. She was a student, just home from school,"* he pauses briefly for effect.

"She was waiting for her brother Marco at a café in the country. She settled at a small table in the corner, across from the window and close to the music," he adds.

"The piano's mournful melodies could be heard over passing cars, coffee chatter, and the noise of life, coming and going," he continues.

"It was an innocent moment, until a friend of Marco's approached her. What he had to say would change everything," he concludes.

Chase Wrigley straightens up in his chair and exclaims, "Fascinating!"

"Those lines came from four different people—two in the States, one in London, and one in Lisbon," Morgan points out.

"So what happens next? I want to hear more!" Fielding exclaims.

"The story continues," Morgan replies.

"For how long?" asks Hadler.

"For as long as we say or until it reaches a natural ending," she explains.

"How do you monetize it?" Hadler asks.

"We thought about that. These stories are so original and so unique, we decided we could compile eBooks and perhaps sell them," she answers.

Brad Fielding has been standing over the laptop, pinching his lower lip between his fingers. He stares intently at the last slide on Percy's computer.

"I've never seen anything like this," he mutters.

"It's really quite unique," says Wrigley.

"How do you control the cadence of the contributions? What if people use profanity? And what if someone is just a bad writer?" Hadler asks.

"All good questions, which we've already considered. This thing is so popular, and the response is so overwhelming, that we'll ultimately need a quick and efficient editorial review process to make sure things are clean, sensible, and well-timed," Morgan responds.

"Kind of like an editorial hold that sometimes accompanies electronic PR or open-comment forums," Percy explains.

"I like it," admits Brad Fielding.

"Me too," adds Wrigley.

"I have a lot of questions, but if this thing can be properly controlled, it could be picked up by one of the large social media outlets," Hadler says.

Morgan doesn't hear what's said next. There are too many echoes bantering inside her head, tangling with recollections of her lifelong love affair with words.

A cacophony of voices, stories, tales and narratives quickly flood those in-between places where memory meets waking dreams. She hears Shakespeare, Hugo, and Wordsworth, and thinks for a moment that she has opened up a portal into human discourse that perhaps transcends time.

The muted voices from the many books, plays, and poems that she spent the majority of her years reading, teaching, and reciting, now represent the footnotes of her life. She recalls the odd placement and size of the countless textual citations that she pulled from history—how she struggled to type them on her mother's typewriter—the Wite-Out®, the onion skin, the half turn of the taut paper pressed tightly against the black strike spool. She could never remember the difference between subscript and superscript; nor could her Smith Corona.

Yes, she'd read, memorized, and recited so very much from the scribes of the Renaissance, the Romantics, the Victorians, the Modernists, the Existentialists, the Beat Generation. But literary periods and movements have been no match for progress. So many words, lessons, and conventions of language have all but disintegrated into the hollow keystrokes of history.

"What a piece of work is a man! How noble in reason! How infinite in faculty!" said Hamlet. Man is a piece of work all right! And our reason and faculty have rationalized us into twenty-first-century brutes, once again communicating in crude symbols. Perhaps hundreds of years from now in some buried room, the people of the future will find an "unfinished" text message and marvel at how very ineloquent we were.

Storytelling, after all, is the original social media since it embraces the very first social movements. Our various accounts of life's events have soothed men's souls since the beginning of civilization.

Aristotle once said, *"When the storytelling goes bad in society, the result is decadence."*

Today, the speed of technology has led to a type of linguistic debauchery where we now advocate acronyms, abbreviations, and broken speech. It's all about brevity and limitation. It's about speed and ease. In the process, our intellectual standards have dissipated into a cyber gumbo that lacks consistency, creativity, or composition.

"Fill your paper with the breathings of your heart," said Wordsworth.

What William didn't know was that paper would one day be gone, superseded by a liquid crystal display that would hold all the ramblings of a simulated world. The real tragedy would rest with the human heart, which has been beating for centuries, only to now languish somewhere in short-lived, electronic chirps.

Our only hope and saving grace is to rally those raconteurs among us to continue to tell our fascinating human tale. Perhaps Victor Hugo had it right when he said, *"A writer is a world trapped inside a person."* It is, after all, a calling. Writers are the mirrors of our time, with something so pressing to say that their only relief is to write it down. So this, then, is a call to arms. A grand charge. A mobilization!

"You can't stay in your corner of the forest waiting for others to come to you. You have to go to them sometimes." Alas, Winnie the Pooh understood the urgency of *going to them*. He was forever going to and fro, looking for snacks and meaningful conversation with Owl, Piglet, or Rabbit.

How would we acknowledge and preserve Hamlet and Aristotle, Wordsworth and Hugo—and Pooh? Would this app be the way? Were these three men before Morgan her Owl, Piglet and Rabbit? Were they there to help her find meaningful conversation?

"Morgan? Did you hear the question?" Percy's voice shatters her waking dream.

"How do we scale this?" Hadler repeats.

Morgan is suddenly rejuvenated, as if her two-thousand-year mental jaunt gave her a much-needed respite from the throes of modernity.

"I'm glad you asked," she jumps in, suddenly very alert. "As I mentioned, we'll sell eBooks. And since they'll likely include writers from every part of the world, we'll have instant, global distribution!" she exclaims.

"That's clever," Chase Wrigley says.

"And the beauty of eBooks is no printing or publishing costs," adds Percy.

"There could ultimately be paperback rights, and even movie rights. These stories are so good, Lord knows where they could go," Fielding predicts.

A pregnant silence ensues. The anticipation is too thick to be cut with a knife. It will need to be sawed back and forth a bit with a serrated edge, just to get through the expectation of the next question.

"So what do you need?" Hadler prompts.

"It's still conceptual at the moment. We need a test environment to prove this will be the greatest creative dialogue and the most intimate human conversation since the creation of the telephone," she replies.

"Would you mind stepping out into the hallway so we can have a quick conversation among ourselves? It would just be a few minutes," offers Fielding.

"Absolutely, gentlemen. By all means, please discuss it. We can come back later if needed, or at another date," she responds.

"Just give us a few minutes," states Wrigley, smiling and pointing toward the door.

Morgan and Percy exit THE FISHBOWL and close the door behind them. The long and narrow corridor has no chairs, plants, paintings, or the typical business trimmings associated with the corporate America of years gone by. Ironically, this new environment of minimalism and emptiness is not only a school of design but also a mark of prosperity.

They walk several feet away from the door and stop. Morgan leans against one side of the hall and Percy props himself up on the other.

"So, did you go blank in there, Morgan?" he asks.

"You know, Percy, I went where I always go when I'm thinking," she replies.

"A little day trip?" he quips.

"Sorry. It came at an awkward time. I got caught up in the drama and intensity of the moment. Whenever someone asks me those big-world questions in the form of fussy little adverbs like "Why" and "How," I tend to retreat to this place of internal outrage, and all I can do is recite literary passages in my head," she tells him.

"No worries. That's why I'm here . . . to fill in the gaps and add some noise to the silence," he assures her.

"You do it well, my friend," she says, smiling.

"So what do you think?" he asks.

"I think we did the best we could," she answers.

"I suspect they'll either pass outright or move full steam ahead, and likely decide on it today," he offers.

"That's so optimistic of you, Percy!" she exclaims.

"Well, I think this is either a *Go or No* type of thing."

"I'm a little worried about Hadler. What about you?" Morgan asks.

"Yeah, he's the money guy. The monetizer."

"He's so combative," she says.

"I think it's his job to ask questions and, clearly, to give his nod to any capital expenditures," he tells her.

"We didn't really talk money. I mean, they didn't give me a chance to say what we need or want . . ."

"Morgan, I think we said enough. They get it. Don't worry."

Back in the conference room, the three businessmen are huddled together at the table. Hadler scratches some numbers on a piece of paper as Chase Wrigley looks on and Brad Fielding walks around the table.

Fielding looks at the other two and sighs. "I just don't know if you can view it that way. This thing is so different," he says.

"Different good or different bad?" Hadler asks.

"I've never seen anything like it, and I agree that it doesn't fit our standard ROI metric. But there's something compelling about it," Fielding says. "It's sexy."

"Sexy? It's not lingerie, for God's sake," Hadler exclaims.

"It's inspiring, without a doubt, but is that enough for us?" asks Wrigley.

"Do you think it's inspiring, Hadler?" asks Fielding.

"Well, it's certainly not another restaurant app," adds Hadler.

"Are you guys worried we may not recoup our development costs?" asks Wrigley.

"Should we care? Imagine a Silicon Valley company getting behind a literary renaissance. We could change the way the world communicates—just like radio, film, and TV did. We could lead the charge to reconnect Millennials with language and use technology to make communication better, not just faster," Wrigley declares.

Hadler looks at him and laughs. "What? Are you going soft on us?"

"We already did all that didn't we?" Fielding chimes in.

Hadler leans down and whispers to both men, "Will the Millennials care? I mean, they can grunt in this town and make six figures, as long as they can press buttons."

"We'll make them care," says Wrigley. "We have to make stories hip."

"So we should be woefully underfunded and needy," notes Hadler.

"It has to be cause-based. Everybody likes causes," Wrigley says.

"Let's see . . ." Fielding ponders aloud. "'Going green' is taken. Saving the wetlands has been done, and everybody's already fighting global poverty."

"But no one is doing this," says Wrigley.

"What do we call it?" asks Hadler.

Fielding doesn't hesitate. "I liked her title, World Wide Writes."

———————●———————

Back in the hallway, Morgan and Percy are silent. Both stare at the floor. Percy is thinking about the last time he ate—the cereal and yogurt from this morning are long gone. He's dipping into his reserves now. It's funny how free hotel breakfasts never seem to keep you full. Is it the child-size yogurts, the mini-bagels, or the itty-bitty cereal boxes that leave one so famished? He's not certain, but an adult-size burger or sandwich sure sounds good right now.

Morgan is busy rationalizing either outcome. If it's positive, she'll shift into high gear. She'll map out precisely how this thing will work. There must be editorial review, submission parameters, global engagement, and story editing. Could they do it alone? What if it goes viral? What if it doesn't? She has so many questions and keeps getting ahead of herself. If they opt not to build her app, she's already decided she'll go back to the "greasers," as Billy Joel once declared, to continue her life as a corporate writer. It was a painstakingly anonymous and comfortably numb existence. Pink Floyd's refrain starts up in her head:

> *When I was a child*
> *I caught a fleeting glimpse*
> *Out of the corner of my eye.*
> *I turned to look, but it was gone.*
> *I cannot put my finger on it now.*
> *The child is grown.*
> *The dream is gone.*
> *I have become comfortably numb.*

Morgan didn't need to be famous. She didn't need to be recognized. She took quiet solace in just being heard. People read her work. They experienced her thoughts. They shared her connections and perspectives about existence—to the extent she could convey them under someone else's name. She knew some authors toiled away late into the night—with bleary-eyed allegiance to the page—and never got that far. They wrote with the hopes of an audience that never came. In many cases, their words never met another set of human eyes. She was one of the lucky ones, and she was thankful for that.

Morgan's thoughts are broken by Brad Fielding's droning voice. His small head emerges from the conference room door as he looks down the hall.

Morgan and Percy straighten up against the wall and look up at him.

He nods, smiles, and utters, "Let's do this."

CHAPTER FOUR

The very next morning, Morgan and Percy are in a Silicon Valley coffee shop called *Zombie Runner*. They're joined by Rowley Gaines, a senior developer at App Storm. Rowley is the type of guy who, at any other moment in time, would be a complete and utter outcast. He's the weird computer dude everyone knew in school who talked endlessly about free space and defragging. He's the oddball tech-centric who girls giggle at when he tells ill-advised stories about zipping and unzipping, routing and encryption. He's the strange CPU creature who never knew how to dress or bathe or find a toothbrush, but in today's world of geek millionaires and twerp tycoons, he's an unsightly genius. Through some wrinkle in time, he has become trendy.

Rowley's a bit on the soft side; pale, pasty, rumpled—clearly an indoor organism. He has a prominent nose on which he wears round glasses, and sports a fashionable soul patch just under his lower lip. He downloads life in neat little bytes and draws the line at backlit keyboards, which he declares are for wimps.

As Rowley sits with Morgan and Percy, his hands move across a small laptop touch-screen as deftly as a maestro conducting Bach's *Brandenburg Concertos*.

"So what do you want the word count allowance to be? I can set it to anything," he queries.

"That's funny," Morgan muses. "We've reduced life to counting words. I remember when there never seemed to be enough words. What's standard?"

"When I was a kid, I used to count cars on the freeway. It made the time go faster on those long trips with my parents. I hated being in the car. We weren't allowed to talk," Rowley says with a far-off look in his eye.

"Anyway," he continues, "I'm going to set up World Wide Writes as a character-driven template, much like Twitter. I'm formulating a five-hundred-character parameter, including spaces. That should give your storytellers about seventy words or about five or six sentences."

"And how will it function? Will it sit on a social media platform?" Percy queries.

Rowley smiles widely and sits back in his chair. He starts to giggle in a perplexingly high-pitched tone, rocks back and forth, and then periodically pulls on his small soul patch to calm himself.

"It's not shackled to a platform. It's free like a bird," he says.

"So it's in a cloud?" Morgan wonders.

"It's intuitive software, on-demand stuff, and the repository is the great expanse of the universe," he replies.

"So is it ready?" asks Percy.

"Can we try it out?" Morgan adds.

"Just let me do a few more queries and then we can take it on a test run." Rowley comments.

Rowley proceeds to tap keys in a rapid-fire sequence of technical mastery. As he types, his mouth moves and contorts, silently sifting through codes in his head.

It would be an amazing thing to witness if it wasn't so difficult and unpleasant to watch. Percy glances over at Morgan, who studies Rowley with the same sense of apprehension and dread.

This madman-turned-genius held their dreams in his somewhat untamed mind, and on the tips of his long, white fingers.

"I think we're ready!" Rowley announces.

"Let's test it!" Morgan exclaims. "How do I get on?"

"I set it up so you can access it from anywhere . . . Facebook, Twitter, Pinterest . . . The story moderator simply has to get it started—by solving the riddle I built into the system," he tells them.

Percy rolls his eyes. Rowley lets out another cackle and laughs out loud.

He explains, "The riddle functions as a key, and when it's entered correctly, it triggers the app-deployment mode. Once the moderator answers the riddle, World Wide Writes is up and running."

"Okay. What's the riddle?" Morgan asks.

Rowley chuckles and looks around the room before whispering across the table, "What has four wheels and flies?"

"*Chitty Chitty Bang Bang*!" Percy blurts out.

"What?" Rowley asks.

"The flying car? Dick Van Dyke?" Percy petitions.

"Julie Andrews?" Morgan adds.

"No idea, man," Rowley shakes his head slowly. "Was that, like, a cartoon or something?"

"We're old, Percy," Morgan declares.

"No, I think Rowley is simply too young," he replies.

"A flying car prototype was unveiled this year at the Vienna technology show," Rowley says. "I just saw a video on it."

"Really?" Percy's eyebrows go up.

"Yeah, AeroMobil," he exclaims. "It can go, like, five hundred miles. It has wheels in the front and back, and moveable wings set in a lightweight, carbon and steel frame."

"So, is that it?" Percy asks. "Who's going to guess that, Rowley? Seriously!"

"No, that's not the answer," Rowley says with a grin. "I just thought it was cool."

"I'm starting to get irritated," Morgan declares.

"Look, Rowley. As fate may have it, you hold our dreams for this wonderful storytelling app within the confines of your goofball, techie, and wonkish little mind," Percy states. "Now, I don't like your laugh, your clothes, or your facial hair, but I need you to get this thing launched!"

"Guys, guys, relax." Rowley's hands rise up in surrender mode. "I was looking for a simple garbage truck."

"A garbage truck? I don't get it," Percy exclaims.

"What has four wheels and flies?" Rowley laughs.

"*Flies* as in *buzz, buzz,*" he cackles again.

Morgan's losing patience, "Let's worry about the riddle later, please. I'm eager to get this up and running. When can we do it?"

"Now, if you want . . ." Rowley replies.

"Right now?" she repeats.

"Yep, right now . . . as in, at this very moment," Rowley nods.

Morgan looks at Percy. She takes a swig of coffee and then fixes her hair. She rolls her shoulders and clears her throat. Percy also takes a sip of coffee. He stretches and decides to breathe out of alternating nostrils. He takes a quick walk around the coffee shop as Rowley and Morgan watch him intently. He finally returns to the table and nods.

"So, you want to go now?" Rowley asks.

"Yes. Don't you think?" she asks.

"It's your app," he answers.

"Yes, now," Percy affirms.

"Do you have a first story line?" Rowley asks.

Morgan starts rifling through her briefcase, picking up one sheet of paper after another. She examines each only to toss them back. She then pulls out a folder and flips through it and tosses that back, too. She now pulls out a notepad.

"Here it is!" she exclaims. "Are you ready?"

"Let me have it," Rowley replies.

Morgan takes a deep breath and slows herself down. She calmly reads, *"A pair of brand new, black designer pumps—Prada or Valentino—size seven, were sitting by the side of a lonely California freeway, as if someone had just stepped out of them."*

Rowley types as she speaks. Morgan and Percy watch him eagerly.

"*Prada* is p-r-a-d-a?" he asks.

"Yes." says Percy. "Capital P."

"And *Valentino . . .*" he adds.

"Spelled just how it sounds!" Morgan blurts out. "Capital V!"

Rowley taps on a few more keys and then declares, "Okay! It's off. Gone, gone, good-bye!"

"Amen, brother!" Percy exhales.

"Okay, just because the app is launched and we have our first story line out there doesn't mean people will come. We have to tell them about it," Rowley reveals.

"How do we do that?" Morgan asks.

"No worries. I'm doing that now. I have my ways." Rowley smiles and chuckles as he taps faster and faster on his laptop.

"I'm not sure about all that you cyber guys do, but anything you could do to help us will be appreciated," Morgan offers.

"I need a coffee. Can I buy you both a 'job-well-done' coffee, latte, or café au lait?" Percy asks.

"Absolutely, old man. I will take a *Mocha Cookie Crumble Frappuccino*, if they have it," Rowley says.

"I'm too old to remember that, but I can get you a plain *Frappuccino*," he answers.

"That works," Rowley replies.

"Okay. So, Rowley, tell me how we'll know when someone writes a line. Where do we look to see if people are starting to build the story?" she asks.

"First of all, you'll get an audible chime, and the new line will appear on the screen of any of your devices for about five seconds. Then you just have to go to your icon and right click it for your story directory. It's called *Pumps*. You'll find this story in there, and the dashboard will tell you exactly where it's at, how many active authors are involved, their locations, their log-in names, and the story's last activity," he tells her.

Percy returns to the table carrying an array of frothy, cream-filled drinks. As they toast the launch, a chime is heard coming from Rowley's laptop. The trio turns to look as a line pops up on the screen:

Her name was Arianna Chaparro, and she had gone to the Nuevo Paradiso Café, deep in California's Coachella Valley, to meet the man she was to marry. In her black evening dress and new fancy pumps, she entered the cantina with cautious excitement, but Gustavo Aurelio was not alone.

The line came from Bedford-Stuyvesant, Brooklyn, from a contributor named Sammie Ocello.

Percy and Morgan look at one another, then they both look at Rowley.

"Cool!" he says. "We're on our way."

"Bedford-Stuyvesant!" Morgan exclaims.

"We need to throw down another line," Percy says anxiously. "We've got to keep it going!"

"Well, it's not really momentum-based," Rowley explains. "But, if you had a next line, now would be a good time to add it."

"I'm thinking," Morgan replies.

At that moment the chime sounds again. They turn to the small laptop as another line of text appears on the screen:

Arianna checked her hair and face in a small pocket mirror at the door, as a Negra Modelo sign bathed her face in bar light and animated her dark eyes and broad lips with old-world radiance.

Maria Moreno, of Bogota, contributes this line.

Morgan flips through her notes as the tone sounds again and another line appears:

She stood against the bright green door, moved across orange walls, stole past purple chairs, mariachi horns, and jam-packed tables teeming with men and women, tortillas, and hot bowls of salsa.

This one is from Simon Lawson in Birmingham.

Rowley suddenly types something on this laptop. His fingers move rapidly as he enters codes and then taps the tabletop, waiting.

"What are you doing?" Percy inquires.

"Checking the queue," he responds.

"Is there one?" Morgan asks.

"Oh, my," Rowley states.

"What?" Percy asks.

Rowley leans back in his chair and shows his screen to Morgan and Percy.

"What's that?" Morgan asks.

"People waiting to storytell . . . from everywhere," he answers.

"There must be hundreds," Percy states.

"I've just refined it so that we can hold at least forty or fifty contributors in the queue. I assume you'll have to store these at some point? Anyway, any more than that, they'll get a message telling them to try back."

"Is this normal? I mean, what's been your experience with new apps?" Morgan asks.

"This is a soft launch—and this, my friends, is huge," he replies.

The tone signals yet another contributor:

As Arianna pushed deeper into the cantina, it got hotter and more crowded. More food and more shots of Herradura passed between overdressed Latinos in heavy hats with wet mouths.
—Yaozu Kim, Shanghai

Gustavo was here. She could feel him. He had given her purpose and clarity when she had all but given up on such things. Her life with men had always been soulless and disappointing. He was different.
—Bryce Hunter, San Diego

She searched the room. Her heart spasmed when she saw him through all the noise and confusion. She melted inside as she moved toward him. As she reached the dark corner where he was sitting, he was passionately kissing a large-breasted chica seated beside him.
—Rami Schechter, Tel Aviv

Arianna stopped breathing. She needed to escape, but a group of mariachi players in silver-trimmed black bolero jackets suddenly encircled her with guitars, trumpets, and violins in a soulful rendition of "Volver." The mournful trumpets blared across the cantina. As hot, boozy men reached for her across wobbly tables, she pushed past them to the cantina door.
—Piero Natoli, Florence

Racing through the parking lot, Arianna suddenly found herself at the edge of the roadway. Everything was silent except for the muted thunder of cross-country trucks on the interstate, powering their way east toward Arizona. In between the larger clatter came the smaller

whispers of the electric waterfall of the nearby casino, which spilled frantic light into the night air, fracturing the desert and making Arianna part of the curious tapestry of love, life, and fortunes lost and found.
—Wendell Brower, Atlanta

Without looking back, she dispassionately stepped out of her shoes and walked off into the night, disappearing down a dark stretch of lonely California highway . . . utterly barefoot and broken.
—Sean O'Driscoll, Belfast

Morgan, Percy, and Rowley remain huddled around the screen.

"This is amazing. Can you pause it?" Morgan asks.

"You don't want to do that. There are more and more lines coming in from everywhere. They're embracing this story dudes," he answers.

"This restores my faith in humanity." Percy states. "Who knew there were so many people with so many amazing mental images and creative thoughts?"

"It's like we said, Percy. Storytelling hasn't really gone anywhere. Everyone has just been waiting for that one platform where they can share their narratives once again," she maintains.

"Well, it appears you've found one," Rowley beams. "From what I can see, this app's hit a sweet spot. We've been out under an hour, and we have hundreds of downloads, more waiting in the queue, and several hundred contributors. I'll call Fielding and Hadler. This'll make them very happy," he grins.

"So what happens now? Where do we go from here?" Percy asks.

"Well, this has been kind of a free play. Now I'll need to set up some moderation parameters," he says.

"So we'll curate what gets posted going forward?" Morgan asks.

"Correct. Then we'll have a hard launch with PR, ad spend, affiliate deals, and partnerships to give this thing some serious steam," Rowley answers. He steps outside to talk on his cell phone.

Morgan and Percy look at one another. Neither one says it, but both feel the overwhelming responsibility of a dream come true. Suddenly, the preservation of oral tradition rests on the success of their new app. They alone could secure the future of the storyteller, the poet, the minstrel, and the chronicler in this new electronic age. The resurgence of the written word rests on their shoulders: their ability to moderate, maintain, and sustain new stories—on their new platform.

"Do you ever feel like we go through life with these massive ideological suitcases, Percy?" she asks.

Percy looks at her and smiles. "The kind without wheels or handles . . . the really heavy ones that hold all the sights and sounds of everything we are? The ones we drag in and out of all the rooms of our lives . . . packing and unpacking until we finally decide to put everything away for good?" he asks.

She smiles at him and whispers, "You totally get it."

He looks at her and says, " *'The struggle itself towards the heights is enough to fill a man's heart.'* Like Camus, my heart is full, Morgan, at least until we push our rock to the top of the mountain."

CHAPTER FIVE

Morgan and Percy find themselves back in THE FISHBOWL at App Storm. Things feel quite differently than they did just a day ago. They now have, for all intents and purposes, a hit app. They're the new and unlikely magnates of mobile, the rookie victors of the Valley, the newfangled sovereigns of all things Silicon—if only they could fit that mold. They've read more Faulkner and Beckett than Christensen and Malone. They know little about "accidental empires," "Bill and Dave," or chips, hackers, long-tails, and singularity. But then again, most Silicons aren't familiar with the nuances of "a summer's day," or "a midnight dreary," or "for whom the bell tolls."

Morgan's main regret in all of this has been the passage of so much time. She let countless nights and weekends slip by without writing down her stories. She didn't promote, evangelize, or lobby for them. It's the greatest tragedy and most significant personal heartbreak—such is the danger of dreams.

As her eyes wander around the now familiar objects of this stark conference room—the reclaimed wood table, the ergonomic mesh-backed chairs, the teleconferencing V-hub, the tray of bottled water—she sees Percy trapped in the midst of a blank, faraway stare. To say anything to him would ruin his quiet moment, but they now seem to exist in a world of ruined moments.

"Are you thinking what I'm thinking?" she asks.

"Probably," he replies.

They giggle at the prospect of the creative arrangement of mere words uniting the nerds and bores, the techies and stodgies, the thrill-seekers and conformists, the compliant and the deviant, the classically trained and the digitally programmed. Their new seat in the winner's circle confirms what Morgan had always believed: that without stories, humanity is fundamentally less human. Without stories, there's no comedy or tragedy, no history or allegory, no success or failure, no truth or fiction, and—above all—no miracles, about which C.S. Lewis once said, "*. . . miracles . . . are a retelling in small letters of the very same story which is written across the whole world in letters too large for some of us to see.*"

In the classroom, Percy had always railed against the standardization of thought and the homogenization of expression. He found iambic pentameter all but intolerable and deemed the haiku a form of literary persecution. He never understood why scholars wanted to put the creative imagination into airtight boxes. The visionary mind is so much larger than that. It's the perfect witness to the human condition and the wild diversity of existence. Louis MacNeice called it, *"The drunkenness of things being various,"* which aptly describes the pleasing intoxication of raw experience. It's that euphoria that has allowed the narrative to survive.

But despite centuries of reciting, recounting and retelling, the art of the story is now fighting for its life. It's "tilting at windmills" as cyber technology and social platforms overtake plot, structure, and meaning. Such is the glaring limitation of our newly networked life. Yes, we're all so connected we're disconnected. And for the first time in history, mankind is changing the words to suit the paper. Morgan and Percy now realize World Wide Writes has the potential to reconstruct language, renovate thought, and emancipate dialogue so that everyone can participate in a global conversation.

Brad Fielding, Mark Hadler, and Chase Wrigley enter the conference room, smiling. They put some papers in front of Morgan and Percy.

Fielding begins. "The results of our test were quite impressive. We believe the app is viable and worth further investment."

"It's apparent that people do indeed love stories . . . you have hundreds of downloads already and a queue of prospects all waiting to join in," Wrigley adds.

"We're not sure how long or how deep this slice of story pie is in terms of our development business, but at this juncture we're willing to put some money and support behind it—to take it where it needs to go," says Hadler.

"This is obviously wonderful news, gentlemen. We're very excited about the prospect of moving forward. So what are the next steps?" Morgan asks.

"We spoke to Rowley and, as you know, there's been a considerable response that will require some management and fairly extensive editing. We've identified some folks within our organization who can take over those tasks," Fielding states.

The phrase enters Morgan like a knife—two words in particular: "folks" and "tasks." *What, exactly, are they saying?*

"We're more than capable of overseeing the creative evolution of these stories. And might I add, we feel there should be precious little editing done. We need contributors to add to this story as if it were a page in their own journal, notebook, or diary," Morgan replies.

"Look, we fully expect you guys to come up with opening lines but, in terms of the day-to-day editing, certain standards have to be met, and we're going to control those internally," Wrigley announces.

"The thing is, Chase, Brad, and Mark, we're the creators. Percy and I have been writing our entire lives, so it just doesn't make sense that we wouldn't control the direction of these narratives," she counters.

Mark Hadler pushes the contract in front of them. "Our support of this project depends on App Storm managing all the story content. In addition, anything that you or they write out there in collective storyland is the property of App Storm, as are the resulting books," he states.

"And what do we get?" Percy asks.

"A percentage. Read the deal points. You write an opening line or two and get a percentage of download revenue as well as any resulting affiliate dollars. You'll make a lot of money by doing very little. You could, in effect, retire," Hadler explains.

Percy folds his arms and straightens his back. "I don't want to retire. I don't care about the money. I think I speak for Morgan when I say that we just want to watch these stories take shape, freely and naturally."

"Look, they may be character-limited, but there should be no limits placed on the human imagination. That's the entire point of this app. We've been sitting here raging against the machine and you guys have been nodding your heads, and now you want to put the machine in charge?" Morgan's irritation reflects in her voice.

"Gentlemen, if I may. This app is different," Percy interjects. "This is the anti-app, if you will. It is the antithesis of automation. It turns the impersonalization of the digital age on its head by pulling together all those authentic voices crying in the virtual wilderness."

Brad Fielding stands up and paces around the table. "That all sounds very poetic and, forgive me if I'm not grasping the larger literary metaphors, but I'm a businessman and it doesn't reflect the reality of how things work in a public forum. Stories evolving on shared platforms have certain protocols, and to ensure those protocols aren't breached, there must be restrictions."

"In other words," Wrigley adds, "we can't have any controversy, defamation, or bad press. I'm sure you understand that . . ."

Morgan jumps to her feet. "Of course not! This is *not* about denigration of character. It's about *telling stories*, for God's sake!"

"Good, then we all agree that we have to prevent hate-speak, cyberbullying, race-baiting, or politically insensitive or incorrect language," says Hadler.

Percy now stands up as well. "No one is talking about race or bullies or politics! We've been doing this ourselves for two years and nothing like that has *ever* come up."

"Well, now you're not doing it yourselves, and we can't take the chance that some wacko won't get on there and start spewing garbage. We need to apply filters and use our own team of sensitivity editors. Anything short of that, and we have no deal." Hadler draws his line.

Percy looks around the room with agitation. He searches Morgan's face, trying to determine what she's feeling in light of these new revelations. She's blank, stoic, and wholly impassive. He looks down at the ground and calmly utters, "That's censorship." He looks again at the three men.

Fielding is tapping his pen. Wrigley is tapping his foot. Hadler is reclined in his seat with his arms folded.

Percy mutters louder this time, "That's censorship! *Je suis* Charlie," and walks out of the conference room.

"What did he say?" Fielding asks.

"I couldn't understand him," Hadler replies.

"Me neither," Wrigley chimes in.

Fielding turns his attention to Morgan. "Surely you understand that we can't make a deal without putting our own protections in place. We can call this quits right now and you'll still retain all the rights to do this thing yourselves, but any development work that's been done is owned by us, and we reserve the right to use it as we see fit," he tells her.

Morgan walks over to the window and stares out at the infamous Silicon Valley, which envelops some of the world's most influential companies and the digital age's brightest minds. This relatively new frontier of sudden start-ups and fast fortunes has all been made possible by a small crystal semiconductor, about half a millimeter thick, that instills machines with logic and memory. This is ground zero for technological advancement—and for the most monumental relinquishment of power and control by the human race.

To the Silicons, life is less about reality and more about the imitation, thereof. It's less about thoughts and feelings and more about computer-generated replications of quantifiable behavior. To the Silicons, communication isn't about words or authorship, but rather logarithms and digital signatures.

The sad tragedy of new frontiers is that they quickly become the worn roads of the overindulged, the thoroughfares of greed, the frontlines of political convenience, and the byways of feigned idealism. For, here, they're always configuring the next thing for our desktop, pocket, or cloud . . . a better way to download, view, or share some wholly unoriginal thought, hijacked from some subtle variation of a more noble past when men toiled in dimly lit rooms with a blank page and a pen. Perhaps, then, Silicon Valley is true to its name.

Morgan turns from the window and looks at the three men, who seem more than confident of their control of the dialogue.

She's suddenly transported back to that cold library hall at Trinity College in Dublin, on the morning of her oral exams. Five men sat across a table, peering over their glasses, waiting for her to answer a question about the significance of Yeats's masterful poem, *Sailing to Byzantium*, within the context of the Irish literary renaissance. Her advisor had coached her not to hesitate, or stutter, or utter certain Americanisms that they found particularly irksome.

Hadler sighs, seems agitated, and shifts in his chair.

Now she was back at Tulane University, in a small tutorial room on the first day of her Keats seminar, when her poetry professor looked across the worn wooden table at five attentive postgraduate women and asked why there were no men in the class. Her mind quickly left the balmy streets of New Orleans and wandered to the stifling summer she spent teaching in a hot modular unit on an Indian reservation in the middle of the Arizona desert.

She had one student she'll never forget. He'd been in tribal prison for killing a man. His final essay was the story of his life . . . and it was like nothing she'd ever read before. A captivating narrative, packed with vibrant words, natural imagery, veneration of the past, reverence for elders, and an abiding sadness for vanquished generations.

It's perhaps the irony of her life that she now sits in a state-of-the-art corporate office in Silicon Valley, before three cyber industrialists, trying to impress upon them the importance of storytelling. But she doesn't see the dialogue as inharmonious. After all, Steve Jobs was inspired by the likes of King Lear, Dylan Thomas, and Herman Melville.

Shakespeare was clear about the imperfection of mankind and the distinctly human tendency to blame our indiscretions on supreme external forces, as illustrated by Edmund, the illegitimate son of the Earl of Gloucester, in *King Lear*.

This is the excellent foppery of the world, that, when we are sick in fortune, often the surfeit of our own [behavior], we make guilty of our disasters the sun, the moon, and the stars; as if we were villains [of] necessity; fools by heavenly compulsion; knaves, thieves, and treachers by spherical predominance; drunkards, liars, and adulterers by an enforc'd obedience of planetary influence; and all that we are evil in, by a divine thrusting on.

Dylan Thomas implored us to reject death; to be rough, wild, and thundering at the end of our days, so we have no regrets—particularly as to our failure to "fork lightning," or to tell our unique tale.

Do not go gentle into that good night,
Old age should burn and rave at close of day;
Rage, rage against the dying of the light.

Though wise men at their end know dark is right,
Because their words had forked no lightning, they
Do not go gentle into that good night.

In *Moby-Dick*, Herman Melville praised the individual merits of the whale. Scholars have argued for generations about whether the beast represents power and independence, or evil and malevolence. It may, in fact, be all those things, since the creature brings out all the persistence and resolve of the human spirit, as well as the weaknesses and the limitations of the human condition.

It does seem to me, that herein we see the rare virtue of a strong individual vitality, and the rare virtue of thick walls, and the rare virtue of interior spaciousness. Oh, man! Admire and model thyself after the whale! Do thou, too, remain warm among ice. Do thou, too, live in this world without being of it. Be cool at the equator; keep thy blood fluid at the Pole. Like the great dome of [Saint] Peter's, and like the great whale, retain, O man! in all seasons a temperature of thine own.

She, Percy, and all those writers waiting for a new way to tell a collective story had found an answer. Now they just need to decide between the easy way and the hard way, the path of least resistance and the one through the wild thicket, and the difference between a prepared story and a spontaneous one.

"Gentlemen, you've given us a great deal to think about. I will regroup with my partner and give you an answer on Monday," she tells them.

"We were hoping for a deal today, Morgan," Brad Fielding offers.

"I understand, but that's just not possible. I need to confer with my partner before making a decision. I must talk with Percy." Morgan draws her own line.

"Our offers are not honored indefinitely, so I suggest you decide whether your app lives or dies fairly quickly," Hadler mutters.

"Whether the app lives or dies is not my truth, it's your reality. Stories will continue to be told. I just have to decide if I can help facilitate the dialogue and how honest I want that conversation to be," she says, matter of factly, and then quietly picks up her things and leaves the conference room. She closes the door behind her, gently but firmly.

———————●———————

The three men sit in silence for a moment. Chase Wrigley breaks the silence. "Well, I'm not sure about you guys, but I wasn't expecting that response."

Brad Fielding tosses down his pen and bolts out of his seat. Hadler stands up at the table.

"Do *not* go after her!" Hadler warns.

"I'm *not*! I'm just standing up. Forgive me if I'm not used to being blown off!" Fielding vents.

"Is *that* what that was? I'm still trying to get my head around her 'truth' and our 'reality,'" Wrigley states.

"Who is she kidding with that idealistic mumbo jumbo? We make more money before our morning coffee than she'll ever see in a lifetime. People like her live and die while I'm deciding how I want my eggs cooked," Hadler spits.

"Here's the thing," Fielding says, as he walks around the table. "The thing about it is . . ."

"What?" Hadler throws his hands up.

"I really want this app," he answers.

"Me too. I have to admit, I think it's brilliant. The world is ripe for it. It has all the stuff that dreams are made of. It's technology to the rescue. It's where the human imagination meets the machine and where tradition finds a modern way to express itself," Wrigley muses.

"Enough, Chase. We get it," Hadler rolls his eyes.

"No, we don't. That's the problem. You think she's going to deal, and we don't," Fielding admits.

"Where's she gonna go?" Hadler asks.

"I agree with Brad. This chick's the type who'd put the entire concept in the top drawer of her nightstand rather than sign something she thinks amounts to a sellout," Wrigley retorts.

"I think she'll shop it and get someone who'll charge her ten grand for a hack job with all kinds of limitations and crap functionality, so the thing never gets off the ground," Fielding replies.

Hadler slams the table. "Listen to you two. You're already in the lifeboats before we've even spotted the iceberg! She's *not* gonna tuck it in the drawer. She's *not* going to shop it. This is her *dream*. Dreams die hard with these literary types. First of all, she's broke. She probably works in a coffee shop or for a nonprofit, saving rainforests or whales. She's gonna talk to her 'sensitive' friend about it and get back to us."

"So what do you suggest we do, Mark? Sit and wait?" Fielding asks.

"In a word, yes. We need to give her time to figure out that she has no other options. Then, she'll be back." Hadler reclines in his chair and folds his hands across his chest.

Chase Wrigley raises his hand, as if in class. "And how long do you think this process will take her? A day? Two days? A week? Two weeks?"

"She said she'll tell us on Monday. Just give her a little time. This is like a poker game. You can't show your hand, and you have to bluff a little," Hadler replies.

The three men slowly leave THE FISHBOWL as the valley outside settles into a post-lunch lethargy. The day's most brilliant brainstorms have since come and gone as groups of product managers now embark on secret trips to Starbucks. The administrative staff pulls plates in and out of the microwave as the marketers crack open Cokes and the programmers sip from bright, orange 5-hour ENERGY® bottles.

CHAPTER SIX

Morgan and Percy are back at their favorite coffee shop. They didn't talk about the app on the long drive home yesterday. They talked about the coastline and the cows, the rolling hills and the architecture, the weather and the traffic. Both knew the app discussion couldn't be brought up casually, it required purpose and clarity. They had to address it with the intention of working through all sides of the issue in order to reach a firm decision. They were just too fatigued. The conversation would require rest and focus. They needed to not be moving.

They both sip lattes and nibble on scones. Morgan glances across the brim of her mug at Percy. He looks tired—not the type of fatigue that comes from too much work or too little sleep, but from being unresolved.

"What do we do, Percy?" she starts the conversation.

Percy sighs and shifts in his seat. "I have no idea, Morgan. I feel like our dream has been shackled, which is a far crueler fate than having it outright killed. What do you think?"

She smiles at him and clears her throat.

"I walked around my neighborhood last night, ready to sign off on this thing and just take the money, but then I thought about the house next door and how it almost burned to the ground several years ago when the junkie son was cooking drugs in the garage. We got his mom out of the house, but she later died. And so did he a few winters later, a victim of exposure, found dead on the back porch. Then I strolled past the tidy two-story home of the lady who'd shot herself because her cancer got so bad. Her husband still sits on the patio alone each night and waves to me with a half-smile. He knows that I know. We all know . . . but no one speaks a word of it.

"And then there's the family who took in two Chinese students, just to make their mortgage payment. Plump, rich Asian kids, with identical haircuts and glasses, who come and go in limos to private schools and ten-thousand-dollar 'day trips' to Rodeo Drive while their American hosts struggle with the daily necessities of middle-class life.

"And, finally, there's the hedge-hidden, ivy-covered house of the old lady who lost her husband to dementia. She's gotten too weak to take out her trash or even navigate her driveway to collect the newspaper. I do that for her in the wee hours of the morning. I've concluded that Ensure® and Rice Krispies® may very well hold the key to longevity. Every so often she cracks open the door and catches me collecting her recyclables . . . and with an odd laugh and a funny nod, offers perhaps the only appreciation that a ninety-six-year-old can muster.

"You see, there's a certain rough beauty to uncensored reality. All these people are characters in a story—and they aren't always pretty, but they're ours. And to remove the grit, or polish up the sides, or smooth out the edges, or make them anything other than what they are . . . would simply be . . . dishonest."

Percy looks up from the table and smiles slightly. "So let's not be dishonest, Morgan."

"Don't get me wrong. Technology has done many wonderful things, but it's also put its thumb in 'our mind's eye.' World Wide Writes is a way around that," she responds.

"Did you know that spiders spin webs from a gland in their abdomen? When their web is finished, they sit in the middle, waiting for a vibration, so they know when to strike their prey," he tells her.

"Are you trying to tell me that we're creating vibrations?" she asks.

"No, we've become the prey, Morgan, all of us," he tells her. "The web has gotten so complex, and the spiders so large, it's impossible not to fall into one of their elegant traps."

"What kind of trap?" she asks.

"Search engines, web crawlers, metatags, keywords, tracking cookies . . ." he recites.

"We're so clever, aren't we?" she adds.

"We've built something so big that it's gotten small," Percy points out.

Morgan shakes her head. "I wonder where it all went wrong?"

"Somebody threw spike strips down along the Information Highway," Percy adds.

"We've got to get around them. We have to take another route," she replies. "I'm not ready to give up on storytelling or poetry or self-expression. Are you?"

At that moment, Rowley Gaines comes bouncing toward them. He's wearing a worn MIT sweatshirt, loose-fitting jeans, and orange sneakers. As he pulls up a chair and sits down, Morgan and Percy look at him with befuddlement.

"Hey, guys. How did it go?" he asks, nonchalantly.

"What are you doing here?" Percy asks.

"Well . . . I felt like taking a drive out of the Valley . . . and I just kind of kept going. I remembered Morgan mentioning this place, and I figured you'd both be here. So how did it go?"

"They didn't tell you?" Morgan asks.

"No. Programmers are always the last to know," Rowley replies.

"Well, we have what appears to be a hit, as you know, and they want to fund the entire build-out," Percy explains.

"That's excellent! Aren't you stoked?" Rowley asks.

"They want us to give up complete control and subject the narrative to web filters, content-censoring software, and a team of editors who will revise everything for political correctness, gender-free usage, and multicultural syntax," Morgan states.

"That's crazy! This stuff is amazing. I've never read anything like it before. It's each person's truth. How can they mess with that?" he asks.

"I believe I have underestimated you, sir," Percy declares.

"So what are you guys gonna do?" Rowley asks, his leg bouncing rapidly.

"We're considering our options," Morgan suggests.

"I think you have to get the app back up as soon as possible. There are people waiting to find out what happens . . ." Rowley contends.

"Apparently, Silicons don't give money without attaching some rather formidable strings, the two biggest of which are power and control. They are the ropes that tie our hands," Percy states.

"We can't allow them to control it. It goes against everything we believe," Morgan adds.

"Then don't!" Rowley says.

"It's their way or the highway," Percy admits.

"No money, no app," Morgan avers.

"I'll build your app!" Rowley offers.

"You work for them; you can't build it. They own everything you develop," Morgan reminds him.

Rowley sits back in his chair and crosses his arms. His leg continues to bounce. "If they paid me. Technically, you're right, but they haven't given me a dime. They let my freelance contract expire last year so they currently have no legal right to the size-seven Pradas, or the *Nuevo Paradiso Café* . . . or to Gustavo and the overdressed Latinos…or to the Mariachi horns or beautiful Arianna."

"They haven't paid you?" Morgan prods.

"Not a dime," Rowley contends.

"You don't have a contract?" Percy asks.

"Not an enforceable one," Rowley replies.

"You would work with us on this, Rowley?" Morgan ventures.

"Absolutely," he nods.

"We couldn't pay you very much," she clarifies.

"I don't want to be paid," Rowley states.

"Nonsense! Everyone wants to be paid," Percy snaps.

"Well, I'm not everyone."

"Why would you help us?" Percy asks.

"I'm not helping you. I'm helping myself," Rowley shrugs.

"Oh, is it a portfolio-building type of thing?" Morgan inquires.

"Not at all," Rowley responds.

"Okay . . . so why would you work on our app for free?" Percy demands.

"The truth is . . . I just want to know what happens…"

"In the story?" Morgan asks.

"I need to know what happens to Arianna."

"You do?" Percy asks.

"I can't stop thinking about her," Rowley reveals. "I keep seeing her, over and over, standing at that café door. I keep hearing the blaring of those horns and smelling the sweat of that crowd and catching that lurid kiss out of the corner of my eye and then seeing her face . . . so broken, so forsaken . . . I want to fix her.

"I want to take her away from that place and those men. I want to tell her that the world is better than that—that *I'm* better than that. I want to put her shoes back on and take her home . . ."

Morgan and Percy stare at Rowley and sit quietly in complete disbelief. Suddenly, he isn't an oddball programmer. He's a human being, perhaps the last person they would expect to be moved by a broken love story. They had pegged him as one of those guys that relishes the solitude of a cooled-down computer room and the company of a circuit board. Guys like him are far more interested in the brains of a CPU than in the emotions of a woman. Today, however, he is sitting in a coffee shop, dreaming of someone who doesn't exist.

But to Rowley, Arianna is very real. She's an unlikely muse in a world where actuality is simulated, life is imitated, and fabrication is a form of virtual flattery. Her vulnerability is highly appealing to a guy who's mastered JavaScript, string processing, and iterative solutions. As he thinks about the silver and turquoise cross around her soft neck, the chandelier earrings that scintillate against her dark hair, and the delicate filigree bands around her perfect fingers, Rowley is overwhelmed by unquantifiable feelings. His face becomes flushed by a pool of pink that gathers in the hollow between his cheeks and jawline.

"Rowley, I think it's wonderful that the story moved you. That's what stories are supposed to do . . . make us feel something. We learn. We experience. We're changed—if only for a moment, or an afternoon," Morgan says gently.

Rowley looks up at Morgan and Percy and smiles nervously. "I don't do relationships, just so you know. On Valentine's Day, I play *Call of Duty*®. On New Year's Eve, I play *Halo*. My Xbox® Kinect sensor is about as close as I get to having someone undress me with their eyes."

"You do understand that Arianna doesn't really exist . . . don't you? She was conceived, designed, and constructed by people across the world," Percy points out.

"Don't we all make up things, Percy?" he asks. "What's existence anyway? Isn't it just a bunch of stuff we choose to believe? Did dinosaurs exist? Did the woolly mammoth? I honestly don't see the difference between what you guys do and what I do. You write stories with words. I write them with code. I won't question you if you don't question me," he replies.

"Fair enough," Percy mutters, shaking his head.

Rowley leans on the table to elaborate. "You see, no one ever crossed a café for me. I never broke a heart or drew so much as a second thought or an errant tear. I'm not a handsome man. I can't toss a ball very well or run overly fast. I can't light up a room with a smile or a clever quip. I can't strike up an interesting conversation, let alone tell a great story.

"And I could absolutely never even hope to navigate a dark corner of a roadside lounge with a big-breasted *chica* or a woman like Arianna. This is it for me. Your app is as close as I'll ever get to the only thing that really matters to me now . . . what happens next."

"Then let's get going," Morgan says.

"How quickly can you bring the app back online, Rowley?" Percy asks.

"Very quickly," he answers.

Rowley pulls his laptop from his briefcase. He turns it on and taps rapidly on the keyboard.

Percy jots down a note and pushes it across the table to Morgan. It reads: *Is this guy for real?* Morgan casually pens a response: *I sure hope so!* Percy laughs aloud.

Rowley suddenly jumps up from his chair and yells, "I'm in!"

"Excellent!" Morgan declares.

"Can we pick up where we left off?" Percy asks.

"The last line was from a guy in Belfast. *'Without looking back, she dispassionately stepped out of her shoes and walked off into the night, disappearing down a dark stretch of lonely California highway—utterly barefoot and broken,'*" Rowley recites.

"Okay, what's the next line?" Percy asks.

"I have it," Morgan says. *"'Arianna's size-seven black Pradas remained there just off the freeway and beyond the casino lights for countless summer days and long summer nights as high rollers and low rollers passed by en route to their destinies.'"*

So now, there's no famous Valley to embrace them, or state-of-the-art office to showcase them. There's no budget or bankroll. There are no teams of programmers, engineers, system architects or designers. Morgan, Percy, and Rowley are going it alone. They're pursuing a story for its merits and possibilities. They're unraveling the narrative of the day and exposing its pale underbelly. They're fighting for life without a filter, and rallying for honest words stirred by the breath of literary heroes who have rejected all convention, and rebuked all limitation.

They're doing what the Silicons warned could never be done. It's a classic flaw of the nouveau riche, the parvenus, and the social vulgarians to forget what is no longer convenient—like the days when dreams were configured in old garages or dorm rooms. Morgan, Percy, and Rowley are forgoing the standard fare, choosing instead to leave the safe harbor. They are, no doubt, anxious. But they realize the pursuit of a dream requires a healthy dose of fear and apprehension.

CHAPTER SEVEN

As the trio sips coffee, they watch the small laptop screen and listen intently for sounds of creative life.

"Where is everyone?" Morgan asks.

"Since we went dark for so long, we lost what traction we had. There has to be a new engagement period," Rowley explains.

"What does that mean, Rowley . . . in English?" Percy asks.

"It means, we have to gain some new exposure, tap into fresh demand, and ultimately secure the type of momentum that will make this app sing."

"And how long will all that take?" Percy asks.

"I honestly couldn't tell you," he answers.

"You know, there was an editor at the *The New York Times* named A. M. Rosenthal who coined a powerful quote for days like these," Morgan offers. "He said, '*Be fanatics. When it comes to being and doing and dreaming the best, be maniacs!*'"

"That sounds good to me. I could be a very good maniac, if provoked," Percy winks.

"That may not be necessary. I believe we have the next lines coming across right now," Rowley says with a smile.

They huddle around the laptop once again as a flurry of words streams across the screen. Rowley silently mouths the word *wow*. Morgan slowly cracks a smile. Percy claps excitedly.

"I'm going to read these precisely as they've come in. I'm going to leave off the contributors, so we can just embrace the story," Rowley states.

"Certainly. We can add them back in later," Percy says.

Morgan inhales a short breath. Percy takes a tiny bite of his black currant scone. Rowley sips at his coffee and then reads the new story lines:

Even abandoned, they were still every bit the pair of dress-up pumps. Unlike the arid landscape, these shoes refused to be reclaimed by the wind, the dust, and the parched earth. Instead they called from the I-10 roadside to be found.

Just beyond the unfinished footpath, the dark shoes danced in absentia as Corinne Barnes passed by. A call center manager on a stopover from Phoenix, Corinne was an early riser and an avid jogger.

She paused over the glossy black pumps and looked all around them. She stood beside them and glanced across at the Nuevo Paradiso Café, now clamped down and boarded up. It must have once been quite the place, she thought . . . quite the place.

Thirsty desert vegetation pushed through the cracked fissures of the abandoned parking lot. The parking paint was faded yellow. Loose wrappers clung to a temporary hazard fence as two dry Corona bottles clinked and rolled with every burst of hot, dry wind.

Corinne pulled each shoe from the earth with the care and curiosity of a skilled archaeologist. Sand slid off the leather cleanly and effortlessly. The Pradas were in perfect condition and must have once complemented the perfect little black dress.

Corinne was no stranger to nice things. She had a custom-built home and drove a new Ford hybrid. She was not one to pick up discarded items, but these pumps seemed different. She felt they had a story.

She tucked them into her track jacket and walked back to the casino. She somehow felt she was carrying someone's life journey. Leaving them behind, she feared, would likely end that journey.

She rolled through the automatic doors of Fantasy Falls. The smell of lit cigarettes, stale coffee, unemptied ashtrays, and old perfume ushered in a different kind of morning—a revelry of glowing screens, ringing machines, and the clanking and jangling of money, coming and going.

Fantasy Falls was truly a paradox. It was where locals came to wager a week's pay. It was where old Indian women rubbed the slot reels with an ancient prayer. It was where travelers would stop to pass the time on a lonely night just off the freeway.

Corinne saw the same broken faces of the drinkers, the pinched lips of the smokers, and the empty wallets of the gamblers. They sat on the same stools, hovered in the same hallways, and convened at the same machines.

Back in her hotel room, she readied herself for a night of dinner and slots with Candy, her lead sales trainer. Candy's life was one in chronic repair. She was forever reinventing herself and existed somewhere between a midlife calamity and a string of endless existential do-overs.

Candy believed in fate and destiny. She felt that life was full of signposts and beacons to help us get through . . . if we could just recognize them when they came along.

She had picked herself up several years back, after living in Paducah, Kentucky, in her Honda, with two kids and two dogs for over six months.

Candy was a survivor and told a powerful story about finding life's silver lining, even if it meant shaking it out of the clouds.

Corinne gently toweled off the black pumps and placed them at the end of her bed. She carefully contemplated them. Who had worn these shoes? Where was this woman going? What made her walk away and why did she never come back? Corinne decided that she must wear them tonight.

Corinne was not a philosopher or a medium. She was not one to channel people or things, but she believed in karma, and the universal principle of cause and effect.

Returning to the casino floor, Corinne moved sleekly in the new pumps across the garish and dizzying carpet, clearly meant to confound the boozy. She studied all the purses and the baseball hats pausing on the backs of vaguely familiar heads, searching the floor for Candy.

Corinne found her smoking by the bar in her Faded Glory skirt and practical shoes. Candy had never been pretty but was once sweet, pleasing, and unintentioned. She now conveyed a nervous loss of control and the urgency of one who tries to manipulate what has been carefully designed to never have order.

Corinne waved, and Candy smiled. They each pushed past the dice-tossers, the slot-stokers, and the filterless-cigarette smokers, and met in a rare opening on the casino floor. Candy called out, "I have drinks at the bar!" as both women moved toward a couple of glasses resting on a tabletop game of poker.

Candy looked Corinne up and down and exclaimed, "Great dress and fabulous shoes! Don't I feel like a frump. What's the occasion? Are we meeting someone I don't know about?"

Corinne smiled and said, "No special occasion. I actually found these shoes. Can you believe that? When I was jogging this morning. They're brand new Pradas. I absolutely had to wear a dress that does them justice!"

"They're gorgeous. Where did you find them? On some rich person's feet?" Candy asked with a snickering snuffle as she dragged on her cigarette.

"On the access road by that old Mexican cantina. They were just sitting there in the sand, like someone had stepped out of them and just wandered off," she answered.

"Someone probably did. My guess is she lost every penny playing Wheel of Fortune® or Double Diamonds and then got dumped. Men suck that way," Candy contended.

She cackled and sipped her drink, a vibrant, red Chelada—a cultish concoction of Budweiser®, Clamato®, Tabasco®, and Worcestershire, which she claims not only prevents hangovers but cures them.

Candy was the quintessential sales person. She was single-minded and iron-willed. She had learned discipline during her early years in the military as a Navy Explosive Ordnance Disposal Technician.

During one deployment, she had an allergic reaction that caused her skin to itch and swell. She never knew what was in that container left at the checkpoint in Kabul, but she was honorably discharged for psoriasis on her knees, elbows, neck, and hands.

She was Corinne's best telerep . . . a real talker with a demonstrable fear of rejection. She was paranoid and controlling, and told big, brash stories that always led back to the sale.

Smoking, drinking, and stress had all exacerbated Candy's psoriasis; and yet a cigarette, a drink, and chronic anxiety were benchmarks of her personality.

The two women grabbed dinner at The Bistro, where they drank coconut drops and ate "Seafood in Crazy Water," featuring lobster, shrimp, scallops, white fish, and mussels in a fennel broth.

After a pair of Almond Joy martinis, they strolled the floor with the somewhat tipsy dream of hitting a Triple-Triple or a Double-Double and living the rest of their life on a Hatteras yacht in King Harbor down in Southern California's idyllic little town of Redondo Beach.

They knew everything was a con here—the booze, the games, the odds. They understood it was unwitting entrapment and a thinly veiled deception, but the chance at change overwhelmed them. Having the worst odds for a shot at a better life seemed fair and worth the risk.

Fantasy Falls had no clocks. Like most casinos, it also had no windows. And yet it made odd overtures of bringing the outside in . . . along with the illusion of leaving the inside out.

The chairs were awkwardly heavy. There was no clear path to the door or the restroom or the cashier. There were just more tables and more carpet, more hands on buttons and cards on tables, and an endless mosaic of backs and heads.

Candy was squinting, smoking, and slouched at a blackjack table. Corinne was perched at a slot machine with a spin wheel. She liked spin wheels. It gave her something to look forward to, other than losing the last of the $200 that she had set aside for gambling.

Corinne suddenly heard an alarm, and her machine was flashing. She looked up at the spin wheel, but it was not moving. What had she won? She looked at the reels and saw three wild cards across them. Perfectly aligned. The Win Meter had the simple designation: Jackpot.

Within seconds a crowd gathered. People stopped, stared, and got uncomfortably close. Corinne looked around at their faces. The expressions ranged from excitement and delight to envy and disgust. She had just gotten what they so terribly wanted . . . a victory against chance.

Candy soon found her way over to her friend. Corinne watched her approach, like an instant replay spliced from a live broadcast. She moved slowly but with purpose. Her gestures were exaggerated, and as she arrived at Corinne's side, she was yelling, "How much?"

Corinne had won $263,091. It precipitated paperwork and signatures and escorts to back rooms where big Indians sat with bigger Indians, watching small screens of crowded tables, countless play buttons, and a hundred hands in a thousand pockets.

Corinne was asked about taxes and lump sums, and then issued a check. It was the equivalent of over four years' salary. What would she do now? Would she stop working? There were so many things she needed and so many that she would like, but all of them she could just as easily do without.

As Corinne emerged from the casino office, Candy was waiting. She was smiling, but Corinne knew that smile. Behind it was resentment and disdain, and in Candy's eyes there was anger. Corinne smiled feebly and then moved past her.

"Where are you going? Let's have a drink!" Candy yelled, spinning around with a double Old-Fashioned in her hand. Corinne stopped, "That was exhausting. I need to decompress a bit. I may go up to my room. I have to digest what just happened," she told her.

"Let me cut it up into small bites for you, Corinne. You won. You did what the thousands of people who spin through those doors can only dream about doing. Winning is what they hope for when they rub machines, swap seats, sip at drinks, and sneak up to the ATM machine."

"I just must have been in the right row, in the right seat, at the right time, and sitting at the right machine. I don't come here with any expectations Candy, and I honestly wasn't paying much attention. Life is so funny, isn't it?"

"Hysterical. You don't have a thing to worry about from here on in, sweetheart. The rest of us will be slogging it out in the trenches, schlepping between desks, working to the bone and on our last nerve to build someone else's dream. Sucks to be us doesn't it, Corinne!" she said.

"I'm sorry, Candy. I'm sorry I won. That was not my intention or my expectation. You understand that this entire place has been meticulously engineered for losing? So winning is simply a happy accident," Corinne replied.

"Yeah, well, that happy accident has made you stinking rich! That happy accident has put you on Easy Street! So here's the thing. I

feel like the fricking Wicked Witch of the West, but I want those shoes!"
Candy declared.

Convinced that the mysterious shoes found in the sand had some inexplicable power over the roll of the dice, the cut of the cards, or the spin of the wheels . . . Candy insisted on wearing them. Corinne removed the shoes in the middle of the floor and walked barefoot to her room.

The shoes were a size too small for Candy, but she crammed her feet into them and approached the first blackjack table, undaunted. This was going to be her night. She put down her money and let it ride.

She drank Rob Roys and Rusty Nails until the table turned hazy and she could no longer clutch her cards because her fingers were numb. Twenty-dollar bills came and went like play money. Cool glasses of Scotch went down like lemonade. With each trip to the cashier, she felt a little more betrayed.

Candy smoked, drank, scoffed, and clicked her heels, waiting for a magic wand to be waved over her or for snow to fall on the casino tabletops to break the spells of her life. Alas, she had never been chosen or blessed or very lucky.

When Corinne came downstairs the following morning, Candy was still at the gambling tables. She was contorted in the chair. Her face was inflamed with booze and bewilderment, and the Pradas dangled on the ends of her toes, over red, bloated feet.

She had scratched her skin raw. Raised and crusted scales had erupted on her elbows and on the back of her neck. She looked at Corinne with a side squint and a dry, crooked smile, shaking her head and then dropping it. "I lost everything. No more savings. No more retirement."

There was a lesson about luck that Corinne understood, but it was hopelessly lost on Candy. As Ian Fleming said, "Luck was a servant and not a master," and "The deadly sin is to mistake bad play for bad luck."

A man from the casino stood beside Candy. "She is not allowed to wager anymore," he said. Candy peered up at him. "No shit, Sherlock!" and proceeded to push off the table, toss a glass, flick her cigarette, and stumble out of her chair, until she was summarily subdued by security.

Corinne brought Candy upstairs before meeting three men at her suite door who asked them to immediately leave the facility. They were quickly packed and gone without any checkout or departure protocol, or words spoken.

With Candy now sleeping in the car seat beside her, Corinne quietly pulled away from the raining fountains at the casino's main entrance. They passed the adjacent trailer park . . . a jumble of lawn chairs, lean-tos, and satellite dishes.

It was a community of people who had long ago given up the ordinary, and for whom gambling had become a way of life. They wagered their pay and their subsidy checks each day and night in a culture of chance.

As they passed the closed-up Nuevo Paradiso Café, Corinne thought about the shoes. They had gotten lost somewhere in the scuffle, possibly on the casino floor. They had become the collateral damage of Candy's complete and utter disintegration.

CHAPTER EIGHT

Rowley suddenly breaks the silence around the laptop. "I don't care about these women! I want to know about Arianna," he declares.

"Oh, I'm sorry. I think Candy is absolutely fabulous!" Percy counters. "She's so defective and wonderfully flawed."

"Rowley, we need to allow the narrative to flow. This is the world's story, remember? Let's see where they take it," Morgan urges.

"But I want to know where Arianna is. That's why I'm doing this. She's what motivates me," he answers.

"Give them a chance, old boy. The contributors know what they're doing. I trust them. They have no agenda other than to be true to their collective imagination. Personally, I had no idea this would be so wonderful," Percy boasts.

"Can't you guys toss in a line about Arianna? Can't you do that for me? You're the app creators, for God's sake!" Rowley moans.

"Rowley, you have to let this unfold without manipulation. To interfere now goes against the rules of creative engagement," Morgan conveys.

"What rules? I don't remember any rules. I think you're giving creativity too much credit. I think most people just spit back out what you feed them."

Percy stands up. "You are wrong about that, my friend! That's an affront to every poet, novelist, playwright, composer, essayist, painter, or sculptor who has started with nothing but the freedom and raw candor of his or her own observations."

"Look, I know what I know because I learned it, not because I watched the snow fall or the tide roll in," Rowley contends.

"Someone once said, *'I am enough of an artist to draw freely upon my imagination. Imagination is more important than knowledge. Knowledge is limited. Imagination encircles the world.'* Do you know who said that, Rowley? Do you?" Morgan asks.

"Who? You?" he counters.

"No. Einstein," she answers. "The father of modern physics. The master philosopher of science and relativity."

Rowley sighs and sits back in his chair with a pronounced, "Hmph." He looks around the coffee shop as if for the first time. Ironically, there's no "relativity" here. It doesn't matter how fast particles move, or the invariant speed of light. No one is observing anything together. The relationship between space and time seems to have lost context. Has relativity, then, become less "relative?" He's overcome by an empirical epiphany.

Everyone seems so profoundly alone. When did we become so isolated? There are no relationships, no partnerships, no alliances. And above all, no conversations. Cafés and coffeehouses used to be places of song, talk, chatter, and laughter. But now, it's a head-down, detached world of human beings, rotating on different parallels, spinning in different spheres, lost in the nooks and crannies of disconnected thoughts. What, indeed, is this digital revolution doing to us? Rowley is overcome with remorse. What part, he wonders, did he play in this?

"Are you okay?" Percy asks.

"I'm fine. Let's move on. Let's see what happens, okay?" he replies.

Morgan and Percy look at one another and then nod with enthusiasm. Rowley enters a series of passwords and reopens the World Wide Writes portal as more lines of text fill the page. Starting from the top, Percy now reads aloud:

The shoes were indeed left under the casino table, and picked up by the housekeeping staff who had the unfortunate job of tidying up the discarded refuse of the winners and the losers—the spontaneous celebrations, the fallout from the drunks and the brawls, along with the cigarettes left floating in stale beers and cheap champagne.

When no one claimed the Pradas, a staff worker, Elena, put them in her locker. She had been in America for the past year on a temporary worker program. She liked it here but missed her friends and family back in Bolivia.

She was one of the Cochalas from Cochabamba, the fourth-largest city in Bolivia and one with extremes of wealth and deep pockets of poverty, where water and plumbing are comforts reserved for the affluent neighborhoods just beyond the urban ghettos.

To her, California was truly a land of plenty, with an abundance of food, water, sunshine, music, cars, houses, beautiful faces, and bright smiles. It was everything she had dreamed about, and her brief day trips to Hollywood and Palm Springs had changed her life.

But her time in America was up. She would be leaving in a matter of days. She wasn't a talkative girl but her encounters with the people who came and went through the lobby and the guest rooms of the casino made her feel that she had come to know the soul of the country.

Americans came in all shapes, sizes, and colors. But despite their differences, they had an astonishing homogeneity. They sounded surprisingly similar, had the same sense of good and bad, success and failure, and all strived for things that were bigger, better, brighter, and bolder.

Her time at the casino was a lesson in Americanism; its overly appealing side as well as its surprisingly dark side. Her job also served as a lesson in friendship and generosity, personal freedom, and complete self-determination.

But despite walking the casino floor day after day, she had never come to understand the concept of putting money into machines for a chance at nothing. She could not comprehend why men and women would give up prosperity so freely, when it seemed so very hard to come by for so many others.

Alas, Americans accepted the consequences of their decisions. She found them refreshingly unafraid and decidedly optimistic. Their enthusiasm and their uniquely American way to view the world could not be found anywhere else on Earth.

Perhaps those shoes represented that hope, she thought. Perhaps they epitomized the spirit of loss and gain that high-rolling Westerners embraced so casually and yet so fully. She knew, when she saw them on the floor, that she had to have them to complete her journey home.

When Elena boarded the plane to La Paz days later, she was wearing the black pumps and a Betsey Johnson® dress that she had picked up in Hollywood. She felt decidedly modish and triumphant.

Once her plane landed, she filed excitedly off the jetway. Bolivia smelled as she had remembered it . . . like open markets and fresh spices, heavy exhaust and the stale tents of the homeless.

She pushed her way through baggage claim, navigating through and among the slow-moving Bolivians in their dark, heavy clothes with their long, pensive stares.

She finally saw her mother. Mama looked older than when Elena had left. She realized that she had become an old Bolivian woman. Her mother's name, Beatriz, was synonymous with travel, but at just forty-eight years old, Mama had dismissed the thought of ever getting on a plane.

Elena's sister, Isabel, was there as well. She bounced and clapped when Elena emerged from the sluggish, airport-weary crowd. She shouted out to Elena, "Te ves muy bien!" She missed her sister's spirit. Isabel, Elena thought, would love America.

The long four-and-a-half-hour ride to Cochabamba included a few stopping points and less-than-picturesque terrain, but it gave Elena an opportunity to reconnect with her mother and sister. Isabel was eager to hear about America.

She asked about the people, the food, the luxuries and, of course, Hollywood. Beatriz sat quietly in the backseat with her hands clasped on her lap, staring off into the darkness with her deep-set Bolivian eyes, before calmly asking Elena if she was going back.

Beatriz knew Cochabamba was no match for the allure of California, but Elena assured her mother that she was home to stay. Her mother turned from the window with a soft smile and a fast-escaping tear that she quickly brushed away.

Her daughters did not approve of such tears. They were strong, modern, and independent women. They embraced the world in a way that she never could . . . with seemingly boundless energy and possibilities. Bolivia had become a better country in their lifetime.

Beatriz was Quechua, one of Bolivia's indigenous people, who boasted proud Incan descent, but have endured crippling isolation and abject poverty in modern times. She could not deny the impact of her former life and that of her long-suffering tribes.

Beatriz's people were secluded, shunned, and relegated to Bolivia's bleakest and most barren regions in the arid highlands. She recalled lingering feelings of emptiness, partly from a lack of sustenance and partly from a lack of purpose.

Unlike her daughters, she did not venture much beyond the steep hillsides of her youth. Her early life was consumed by the pursuit of food. There was precious time for little else. She went to work at ten years old, selling belts and pottery for a single potato or a cup of corn.

The hunger had been so great that her grandmother taught her how to prepare meals in her mind—big bowls of quinoa porridge, grilled guinea pig, salsa, corn, and colada morada. The feasts that unfolded in her imagination were so vivid, it kept away the pain.

Likewise, working men sucked at large wads of twisted coca leaves, crammed between their cheek and jaw, for energy, euphoria, and an escape from the same pervasive hunger. They chewed until their tongues and throats were numb, and everything seemed a bit more tolerable.

The emptiness was pervasive. Beatriz was from a dry, windswept place of bare hills and gravel roads. It was rugged and remote, with steep climbs or long, difficult walks—a place that either broke you down or that you somehow quietly slipped away from.

Beatriz had met Cedric when she was just sixteen. He had a strong jaw, an easy smile, and an active mind. His dreams went beyond those hills and farther down those roads, well past the confines of the wildly jagged mountains that were at once beautiful and ruthless.

Cedric used to quote Dostoyevsky, who said, "The mystery of human existence lies not in just staying alive but in finding something to live for." Cedric lived for Beatriz. He was a simple man, and a very good man.

Cedric worked in the Potosí silver mine and came home each night with silver dust in his hair, under his nails, and within the pores of his skin. He worked with men from all walks of life and heard their stories. Some were rich men, some were poor men, and others were just passing through.

At night, Cedric described them all as he glistened in the firelight. One would think that a man dipped in silver dust was destined for riches, but that mountain ate men and Cedric died young of silicosis, a lung disease borne of mineral dust. He never got to really know his girls.

Beatriz believed that he gave his life so his children would find a better place, and they did. The day they left the mining village for the last time, the hills erupted in magnificent sunshine, as if Cedric was looking down with his broad mouth and big smile.

Beatriz took the girls to Cochabamba and opened a dress shop, where they grew up in a world of brightly colored skirts, woven sweaters, bowler hats, silver-and-turquoise jewelry, moneyed tourists, and Bolivia's most well-to-do women. What a difference a generation makes.

Beatriz and the girls had a relatively modern flat in the city, not far from a church, a green park, and several restaurants. They were comfortable in Cochabamba. It was a pleasant place with gentle mountains, tame lawns, and hillsides full of carefully cultivated wildflowers.

As the trio prepared for a Welcome Home dinner at their favorite café, Elena once again donned her black pumps. "You must tell me about these shoes," Isabel bellowed. "Did you buy them on Rodeo Drive? How much were they? How long did you save up for them?" she asked.

"I will tell you all about it over dinner," Elena answered. When they arrived at Paprika, it was crowded with urban Bolivians and small groups of colorful tourists: European, American, and Brazilian, drinking fruit daiquiris and eating llama and salmon.

Everyone was well-dressed and vibrant. They hugged, laughed, drank, and posed. They took photos of their meals and of each other. They talked on cell phones and played on tablets. They passed budin de coco, espuma de mango, and helado de canela—local desserts of coconut pudding, mango mousse, and cinnamon sorbet—around long, crowded tables.

Beatriz and her girls had steak and potatoes with tiramisu and coffee. It was good to have everyone back together, Beatriz thought, as *she watched her girls chat across the table. For a moment they were toddlers again playing thunka in the shadow of Cerro Rico, that silver-rich mountain near Potosí.*

"Now the shoes, Elena. They are simply gorgeous," Isabel suddenly gushed. "No more suspense! I want the entire story. Did a man buy them for you? Was he American? Was he rich? Was he a handsome Hollywood actor?" she asked.

Elena leaned across the table, as the candlelight danced in her dark, wide eyes. With a coy smile she said, "I got them at a casino in California. A woman left them under a table. I asked my manager if I could have them, and he said to just take them. So I did!"

Beatriz interrupts her. "Elena, why would you want something that did not belong to you? How could you take someone's shoes? What did this woman have on her feet? How did she walk in the desert?" she asked.

"No, Mama. You don't understand," Elena explained. "This woman was gambling and lost everything. She did not want the shoes. She blamed the shoes for taking her money. When they asked her to leave the casino, she tossed the shoes away."

Beatriz looked at her with anger, and with her chin raised up in condemnation. "To the Quechua, shoes are dignity. When I was a girl, we had no shoes. We covered our feet with rubber and leather to protect them from the rough earth. It was the only way we could leave home and return again. Shoes were our freedom."

"Mama, I did not take the shoes. The woman left them," Elena stated in an attempt at conciliation. Beatriz spooned her tiramisu. She was disappointed. She was clearly uneasy about these mysterious, high-priced, fancy heels.

Elena glanced at Isabel, and both girls smirked slightly. They loved their mother, but her life had always been defined by all the things she never had. She came from a world of hardship where a bag of barley, a woven blanket, and new shoes took on far greater significance than her daughters could possibly grasp.

To Beatriz, everything was a lesson. She reminded her girls about the hunger, thirst, and isolation of Bolivia's poor and, as they left the café in silence, one could hear the gap between the two generations tapping on the pavement along Av Salamanca.

The next morning when Elena awoke in her old bedroom beside a sleeping Isabel, the shoes were gone. She was upset but not surprised. Her story of the casino, the American woman, and the twist of fate that put the shoes in her possession was far more than her mother could accept.

Afterward, at the small table near the kitchen, mother and daughter drank coffee together. Beatriz did not say where she took the shoes, and Elena did not ask. The unspoken conversation between mother and daughter said more than all their phone calls over the past year.

Rowley pauses and looks up at Morgan and Percy. Morgan's hands are clasped about her knees, and her head is tilted to one side. Percy is leaning across the table with his chin propped on his palms. Both are in the "enraptured" posture that one adopts when a story truly engages its readers. They have been swept up by the lives of Elena, Isabel, and Beatriz. From the impoverishment of Bolivia's highlands to the promise and vitality of its cities, like Santa Cruz, La Paz, and Cochabamba, the three Californians are suddenly flies on the walls of an interactive history.

Through the growing cyber narrative, they are witnessing the firsthand evolution of one of the world's poorest countries. One that is as much divided by class, race, and tribe as by tradition, convention, and the crush of modernity.

The café clientele has now rotated and changed. The World Wide Writes trio has outstayed the afternoon coffee quaffers: the poets and parodists, the composers and performers. Evening is approaching and night-crew workers, with that look of needing a pick-me-up, are shuffling in with their drawn faces and drowsy eyes.

Coffee is their panacea and their fix, a therapy of sorts that breathes new life into the various souls that partake. They like everything about it: the smell of grinds and heat, the sound of steam rising over folk guitars, the feel of their fingertips on earthenware grips, their tongues tasting the first sip, the dark concentric rings on the cup-and-spoon-worn tables, and the rush of clarity that helps them find context and perspective on a Tuesday evening.

"Bolivia . . . That's one of those countries you never really think about," Percy utters.

"I have a very specific picture of Beatriz in my head. Does anyone else?" Morgan asks.

"Not Beatriz, but Elena is very clear to me," Rowley offers.

"What does she look like?" Percy inquires.

Rowley looks up at the ceiling and closes his eyes. "She is a small woman with a broad face and wide, dark eyes. She has a prominent mouth and an engaging smile, like her father. Her hair is a deep sable, and it's pulled up away from her face. She's not as much pretty as she's ethnic and emblematic."

"Very nice, Rowley. I believe you've officially crossed over into the world of creative thought. Now Morgan, please tell us about Beatriz," Percy inquires.

"Beatriz wears braids tucked into a dark sombrero," Morgan begins. "She's wholly archetypal. Her bright-blue pleated skirt billows at the waist, just below a cheerful orange shawl made from alpaca wool. Her face is a study in adversity and long spells of hopelessness.

"She rarely smiles but holds the hard lines of disadvantage taut around her mouth. She's quick to tear up and is often overcome by the shadows of her past and the anguish of her tribes. She wipes her eyes with thick, hard-skinned hands and slips a coca leaf into her mouth with large flat fingers, until she can once again conceive of happiness and see the face of God."

"You guys are good. I feel like I know each of these ladies intimately," Percy lauds.

Rowley sighs. "Still no Arianna."

"I think we're getting close. We're going to find out where she went, Rowley. We just have to follow the shoes," Morgan concludes.

CHAPTER NINE

Rowley sighs and points at his compatriots, inquiring about more coffee. Both Morgan and Percy nod their heads affirmatively. They can't stop now. The story of the shoes has crossed continents, and something truly big was about to happen.

Rowley returns to the table with a tray of steaming coffee mugs and a bottle of water for each.

"Hydration!" he exclaims. They sip some water and then some more coffee as Morgan continues the reading.

There was perhaps no better place to discard an unwanted pair of shoes than the Feria de El Alto—one of South America's largest flea markets. The vibrant pinks, reds, and blues of the dresses, frazadas, shawls, polleras, capes, and ponchos overwhelmed the senses.

It was a jungle of color and danger, packed with pickpockets, purse-snatchers, swindlers, and charlatans. There were stolen goods, borrowed goods, and half-used goods. There was third-world garbage, new-world contraband, and an occasional treasure for those seeking something homespun and rustic.

Crash Winslow came to Bolivia with a friend who buys traditional garments, sandals, and quilts to sell back in California. After a few days at the market, they'll return to Ilha do Mel, an island off the coast of Brazil, and the closest thing to paradise for avid surfers.

Crash was not the typical shaggy-haired adrenaline junkie but instead, clean-cut and tidy, clear-eyed and watchful. He had a solid, sturdy frame under a snug LSU Tigers T-shirt. He smacked of sobriety and self-control. One quick glance, he could be ROTC or active military.

Crash was raised by a God-fearing Southern woman who held tight to Scripture, and even tighter to her kids. The Bibles of his youth were well-read and well-worn. He had turned the other cheek so many times he could barely face life dead-on.

His buddy Jake, however, was pure California: a tan, golden-haired wave rider. He's a hipster in board shorts, a Pepperdine University grad, a moneyed beachnik, a lord of the sand, a flip-flopping bowl-toker with a lean body and a light mind.

Jake Waring grew up in Malibu. Despite being spoon-fed and mollycoddled, he had a relatively agreeable demeanor. He treasured his independence and craved adventure. He spent his life trying to figure out what he could be or do that did not involve containment.

When Jake wanted to be a golfer, his parents bought him a golf course. When he wanted to be a filmmaker, they bought him a studio. When he caught the surfing bug and the ocean would not name its price, they bought him a surf shop in Venice Beach.

The shop enabled him to take exotic surfing trips and to purchase interesting inventory from all over the country and the world: long boards, short boards, gloves, hats, blankets, bags, jewelry, etc. Above all, it gave him purpose, all the purpose a midnight toker would ever need.

In 2008, Crash and Jake met on Holly Beach, the Cajun Riviera on the Gulf of Mexico side of Cameron Parish, and had been travel-surfing ever since. Ilha do Mel was their fourth excursion together. Bolivia was to be just a "quick" side trip—by ferry, train, air, and cab.

At the Feria de El Alto, the two men marveled at the sheer variety of goods in this primarily indigenous city. The stacks of garments, racks of clothing and oddball things included boxing gloves, silk ties, and sewing machines. Jake came across a stall selling guinea pigs next to one selling human kidneys.

Crash stumbled upon the hallucinogen tent packed with plant-based drinks, powders, smokes, and eats. There was ayahuasca, torch cactus, blue lily, morning glory, and a coca leaf bar with liquor, bowls of sweet leaves, and groups of smiling men with engorged cheeks.

In the next stall, Crash found the size-seven Prada pumps, sitting between some macramé purses and a stack of holiday-themed bow ties. He purchased them for the equivalent of three dollars for a woman back on the island. He didn't even know her shoe size, but he could never forget her face.

Jake ambled up beside him and asked, "What's with the high heels?" Crash smiled and answered, "They're for that girl I was telling you about. You know, the one at the café. They're Prada, three bucks. I just saved about $600."

Jake looked at him with confusion. "Who is she? Cinderella? Why would you buy a woman a pair of shoes? That's not romantic. That's like getting a woman a hair brush or some deodorant. What's up with that, bro?"

Crash replied, "That's not true. Shoes are soulful, pardon the pun. They carry us. They're how we walk about the world and, in many ways, an extension of our personality. Some shoes are a work of art. I actually think that shoes separate us from the animal kingdom."

"Soulful? Animal kingdom? What the hell? Dude . . . how many coca leaves have you had?" Jake asked him.

"A whole bunch," Crash replied. "Along with some of that agwa stuff. I feel awake. I feel conscious. I look around this place and if I change the focus of my eyes just a little, it looks like a LeRoy Neiman painting. Do you know what I mean?" he asked.

The pair left the market, carrying knapsacks and duffel bags stuffed with blankets, scarves, sandals, leather bracelets, puka beads, and an array of turquoise jewelry.

They jumped in a taxi to head back to the airport. The outside of the cab was "old car" blue—the kind of blue one would find on a 1970s Datsun or a Pinto. The windshield was filled with stenciled decals and sales jargon, in cursive window paint touting "Fast Airport" and "Style Ride."

The inside of the cab had a velour dashboard mat with bright orange fringe. A small Bolivian flag on a wooden stick was wedged into the air vent. The Blessed Mother hung from the visor, and a petite potted plant was where the radio used to be.

The backseat was unyielding steel mesh, making the fast, narrow roads to El Alto International Airport somewhat agonizing. The rear left-door handle was broken, but held together with rope. The cracked rear windshield was "repaired" with a sticker of President Evo Morales.

As they rumbled through the streets, they passed bright wall art: fluttering wide eyes winking from stacked cinder blocks; Mona Lisa grinning under a bowler hat; a large toad holding a paintbrush; indigenous women shopping; oversized birds flapping; and children with blue, orange, and gray faces, watching . . .

There were portraits of activism and cynicism, satire and revolution, depictions of suffering and rage, parodies and mockeries. There were paintings, murals, graffiti, doodles, and defacements.

The airport was small and resembled a shopping mall, with big antennas and diesel fumes. Crash and Jake successfully stashed their wares and boarded a small plane to Brazil. As the Amazonas jet pulled up from El Alto, a fast fog turned all the bright colors of Bolivia to gray.

Crash pressed his head to the round airplane window. He was suddenly very tired. The coldness of the glass pane helped to soothe the turbines in his head and ease his disorientation. He closed his eyes and floated with the plane.

"So tell me about this girl," Jake said, startling him. "Where did you meet her?"

Crash turned his head from the glass and squinted at Jake with one eye. "I haven't met her. I've just watched her," he replied.

"Watched her? Are you stalking this chick?"

"No. I just saw her once. I haven't even approached her," Crash said.

"Let me get this straight. You saw this girl in a café back on Ilha do Mel. You've never met her and not so much as talked to her, but yet decided to buy her a pair of shoes?" he asked.

"Yes," Crash responded, his eyes again closed.

Jake laughed and shook his head. "What am I not understanding here, Crash?"

"She's not just any girl. You can't help but watch her," he retorted.

"Okay. What does she look like?" Jake asked.

"It's not what she looks like. It's her movement and her gaze. It's how she portions time and space. It's how she holds her hands on the tabletop. It's the way she pulls in air. It's how she waits for something or someone. I would give anything to understand what or who."

"Okay, Romeo, and you intend to do what? Give her these shoes and hope that you turn into Prince Charming or Don Juan?"

"Hardly. She's completely out of my league," Crash said. "I'm not like you, Jake. I don't catch a woman's eye. They're not drawn to me. They don't step out of their life to walk into mine. I'm an average guy . . . a simple Southern boy trying to do a little better than my dad."

"Stop selling yourself short. I bet your dad never made it to Bolivia or Brazil, did he? I bet he never surfed off Fourchon Beach in Grand Isle. Did he?" Jake asked.

"No. No, he didn't surf at all. He worked on an oil rig off the Gulf Coast. He had three kids, and up and died at twenty-six, so that ruled out too much surfing or any extended travel," he stated.

"I'm sorry, dude. I do remember you telling me that. My bad. But just because your dad died young doesn't make you a deadbeat or a washout, or in any way a bad person."

"I was just raised different than you, Jake. I never had expensive boards or lessons. I started surfing because I'd go down to the beach and look for my daddy. My mom said he was too far out on that rig to ever see me, so one day I just started paddling."

"You were paddling out to a remote platform? Are you crazy? Do you know how far those things are? Never mind all the tidal zones and riptide currents. Did he know you were looking for him?" Jake asked.

"I doubt it. He was miles and miles out. The funny thing is, I swore I could see him, especially at night," Crash stated. "That rig was a bright, bright light on the horizon, and he was like an ocean star."

"So he was young, huh? Men with young kids just don't die like that. What happened? Was there an accident? A fire? An explosion?" Jake asked.

"No. It wasn't anything as spectacular as that. He just got sick on the rig, and that was kind of it. He never came home again, and everybody just stopped talking about him," Crash replied.

"One day I paddled and paddled so far out that I got too tired to get back to shore, so I learned how to let the waves take me in. It was the least they could do. After all, they had my dad," Crash said.

"If anyone could have made it out to that rig, it would have been you. You're a good surfer, Crash, I know that much. You're a damn good surfer," Jake told him.

"Jake, if I was a good surfer, you wouldn't be calling me Crash," he said with a smile. "I'm Braydon Zachary Winslow, the second."

"You are, and I bet your daddy is listening to us right now on an offshore platform in heaven . . . watching every run we make and every wave we catch . . . I don't think they ever really leave us." Jake said.

The flight from El Alto to Curitiba, Brazil, was an eternity of some thirteen hours. Jake slept through most of it while Crash faded in and out to the drone of the engines and the shudder of high-velocity steel shredding the vault of heaven.

He hadn't thought about his father in so very long. He tried to remember his voice, but it was gone. It's odd that the tone and echo of a man he could once pick out of a crowded market, or that rose above the noises and banter of Little League bleachers, was now lost.

He hadn't fully come to terms with it. If he'd learned anything on this trip, it was that he missed his dad. When a person loses someone very close, a void forms that can never really be filled. The heart eventually stops trying, and over time simply finds new paths around the pain.

His father was gone because he was unlucky. There's no other explanation. Crash looks over at Jake and doesn't envy him for what he doesn't yet know: that when a man loses his father, he loses his metaphysical footing, and the very scaffolding that supports his soul.

He takes out the Prada shoes from a box under his seat and examines them closely. From their soles, he can tell they had obviously been walked in, but barely. They were only gently used. But why had he bought them? Why did he feel compelled to give them to a woman he had only seen once for a fleeting moment?

The stewardess suddenly rumbles down the aisle with a bumping, clanking beverage cart, as Crash tucks the shoes away. The plane stirs to life with cabin lights and the smell of fast-heated food in a simulated mile-high morning as Jake awakens, asking for coffee.

Crash looks over at him. Even with the creases of sleep and the crinkles of slumber, he is handsome. With a surfer stretch and a wide yawn, he asks, "Did you sleep?" But Crash never slept on planes. He'd never gotten used to the staggering loss of control of 35,000 feet.

From the air, Curitiba appears to sit in the center of a deep-green duvet atop an unmade bed. A tangle of trees and concrete spars at the city's outer edges as a metropolis of Lego-like skyscrapers and neatly stacked suburbs quickly comes into view.

Once they are on the ground, Curitiba becomes a bustling, thriving municipality—a city sprinkled with green spaces, botecos, and pastelarias. It's an ideal place to fuel up before the rather laborious trip out to Ilha do Mel, via train, bus, and boat.

They both looked forward to the enchanting island, a place of tantalizing extremes. A place so beautiful, it's tragic. A place so natural, it's contrived.

A sunny day in Ilha do Mel was extraordinarily bright, while a rainy one was delightfully gray, and the quiet island nights resonated with the deafening noise of nothing.

Ilha do Mel was a place without cars or lights or roads, only sandy trails and old wooden trolleys connecting small villages. There were endless expanses of white sand and rolling waves, surrounding dense forests, natural grottos, and meandering inlets of freshwater marshes.

There was no shortage of inner peace on the island, a special sanctuary known for its prevailing calm. A paradise coveted by surfers, stargazers, wanderers, dreamers, and lovers. And there was, of course, the Enchanted Beach and the stories of the "Charmed Ones," who recount tales of beautiful women and timeless temptations.

Once they arrived, Crash would set out to locate her . . . the breathtaking woman he'd seen for just a moment at the café, slowly stirring her cappuccino and carefully watching the door. If only he could be the one she waited for.

CHAPTER TEN

Morgan stops reading and looks across at Percy, who's now resting his head completely on the table. She then checks on Rowley, who's slumped down in his chair, his gaze firmly affixed to the side of the small silver laptop. Percy's eyes are a luminous pale blue. They're tired around the edges and pink in the corners, the kind of pink that results from staring too long, or concentrating too much, or crying just a little bit.

"Are you okay?" Morgan asks.

"I'm fine. That Dad thing was a bit intense," he replies.

"Did you lose yours?" Rowley inquires.

"I did. A long time ago. It almost seems like a different life now," Percy answers.

"What happened?" Rowley asks.

Percy rubs his eyes and straightens up in his chair.

"He went off to work and stopped at the post office to mail some bills. He had a heart attack. They found him in the lobby, still holding the envelopes . . . his final payments to MasterCard, Macy's, and Con Edison. It's crazy that I had to know. I had to know where he was, what he was doing, and what was in his hand. What was in his damn hand! Nobody would tell me when I asked, but it was important for me to understand what was important to him in the last moments of his life.

"I was just a kid. He would always come and go in silence. I don't think he liked being home all that much. I remember his raincoat on the banister. It smelled like cigarettes and Chinese food. I remember his hat on the hall dresser next to his keys. I remember his large watch on the nightstand. I would put it on and it would slide clear up my forearm. It smelled like aftershave. There are so many things I still want to know about him—what he hoped for, what he dreamed of, what got him out of bed every day. But mostly what he thought about when he sat alone in the dark."

"Sorry," Rowley mutters.

Morgan gets up from the table and rubs Percy's shoulders and then hugs him. She straightens up and looks at both men.

"This has been cathartic for all of us. I'm struck not by the differences of all these contributors but by their similarities. There's a harmony that transcends time, place, geography, ethnicity, and social class. This is a conversation with existence that's as natural as breathing. I'm more determined than ever to keep this going."

"Hear! Hear!" Percy states, waving his coffee mug. "Shall I get another round?"

"So where do you think she is?" Rowley asks, disrupting the moment.

"Who?" Percy responds.

"Arianna," he replies.

"Wherever they've chosen to place her. We may not know until the end of the story," Morgan counters.

"She's at a café on the island, isn't she?" Rowley asks.

"She could be . . . but she could also be in a million other places," Percy counters. "Look, Crash and Jake could hop a fishing boat to Rio next and leave the shoes in the fish hold, where they're eaten by a Bonito tuna and later served up to Arianna with a wonderful lemon caper sauce and a side of linguine at ZZ's Clam Bar in New York."

"I need to find her before they do," Rowley continues.

"Rowley . . . Crash and Jake are characters. You know that, right? I know I keep saying this, but I want to be clear. You know they're not real, don't you?" she asks him.

"And neither is Corinne, Candy, Elena, or Beatriz," Percy adds.

"And Arianna is likely not a real person either. She clearly represents something extraordinary to you, and I want in no way to diminish that—but she was made up, as well," Morgan states.

"So what exactly *are* all these people?" he asks.

"They're personas that exist in the imagination of storytellers who've signed on across the globe," Morgan explains.

"So let me get this straight. You've been railing that the cyber world is simulated and inhuman. You've accused anyone who tweets or texts of being a disconnected sell-out. You've written off an entire generation as incapable of thinking or feeling. And now you're telling me that these stories of yours aren't real?" he exclaims.

"That's not what we're saying!" Morgan retorts.

"Then, what?" Rowley counters.

"Percy?" Morgan pleads. "Can you offer another perspective here?"

"Why, thank you, Morgan," he clears his throat, tugs on his sleeves and responds. "Rowley, we're just saying that we've invited people from all over the world and all walks of life to tell a creative narrative, and since we don't know any of them, we cannot possibly vouch for the authenticity of what they put forth."

"I call bullshit!" he cries.

"Excuse me?" Percy exclaims.

"I need to find Arianna in whatever form she exists . . . virtual, spiritual, or theoretical," Rowley proclaims with an air of desperation.

"I haven't been able to think about anything else. Look, I'm a tech guy," he reminds them. "Programming is my story. I live in a world of data and networks. I prefer numbers to words. I'd rather spend my nights with code than with people. To me, the world is one big file stream. The universe is simply a giant information batch where communication comes in and communication goes out. I don't care what it looks like, or how it sounds, or whether it inspires me. I just care about where it goes and how I get it there. It's a perfectly coherent asylum of structure.

"But now, I've been forced to read these stories of yours. It's not what I do, and it's messed up my head! I'm a mishmash of urges and impulses that I no longer understand. Do you get that? *This is not what I do.* I've been trained to verify information, track source data, and establish statistical origin. So, despite what you say, she's very real to me . . . and now I have no choice but to go to this island and look for her."

His words hung in the air and then landed in the center of the coffeehouse table, amid old spills and stains of lost confessions and quiet inspirations. They echoed against the stacks of ragged books, the worn couches, and the old paintings of people that no one really knew.

How could they possibly explain the rules of human engagement to a man who could not differentiate between reality and fiction?

Morgan offers in a stoic voice, "Okay, so let's say you look for her. Let's say you do what you need to do and go where you need to go. What about the app?"

"I can keep it going from the road. Or show you how to log-in and pull the data stream . . . I mean, the story lines," he replies.

There was clearly no dissuading him. Something had awakened deep inside Rowley that was calling him to shore. It was beautiful and dangerous—only time would tell whether he would shipwreck his soul on Ilha do Mel, or finally find his muse. It was precisely as Morgan has always believed—that art was possible in every man. That stories exist in every heart. As the painter, Robert Henri, said:

> *When the artist is alive in any person, whatever his kind of work may be, he becomes an inventive, searching, daring, self-expressive creature. He becomes interesting to other people. He disturbs, upsets, enlightens, and opens ways for better understanding. Where those who are not artists are trying to close the book, he opens it and shows there are still more pages possible.*

Rowley was preparing to embark on the greatest voyage of his life. Suddenly, nothing mattered more than finding Arianna; a mythical woman built with keystrokes and hyperthreads, suspended in a cybernetic cloud. Maybe she was real, maybe she wasn't. But within the passion of the search, he could finally feel something. Perhaps he could fix his generation in the process, repairing all the damage done by those firewalls and gateways.

His life had been an easy hack. His desires were locked in safe mode, with old passwords, fixed defaults, and self-populating caches. He'd been defragged to the bone, and he couldn't Google or Bing his way back to the human race. He knew that life was about chance and that love was about desire. As Nietzsche said, *"the voice of beauty speaks softly; it creeps only into the most awakened souls."*

And so, Rowley's soul had finally been awakened, and his story was, in many ways, just beginning.

"Well, if there's no pot of gold at the end of the rainbow, or Emerald City at the end of the yellow brick road, promise me that you won't condemn the process," Morgan tells him.

Rowley smiles and gives Morgan an awkward hug. He offers his hand to Percy, who shakes it firmly.

Rowley had never quite looked at existence this way . . . past its numerics, beyond it continuums, and away from its network infrastructures.

They knew they had to endorse his journey. They simply could not lobby for a return to creative expression and yet deny Rowley his creative fantasy. They couldn't question his devotion to Arianna, wherever—or however—she exists to him. D.H. Lawrence perhaps explained it best:

> *No form of love is wrong, so long as it is love, and you yourself honour what you are doing. Love has an extraordinary variety of forms! And that is all there is in life, it seems to me. But I grant you, if you deny the variety of love, you deny love altogether. If you try to specialize love into one set of accepted feelings, you wound the very soul of love. Love must be multi-form, else it is just tyranny, just death.*

CHAPTER ELEVEN

From the air, the beauty of the island sends pangs through Rowley's heart. It's a magnificent sight: lush bouquets of mossy-topped trees; long, foam-lined beaches with a lapping complacency. The island's shape resembles a free-form hourglass having tumbled on its side, engorged itself with sand until it was unable to flow, or to run, or to count time.

He crosses from the mainland on a brightly colored ferry, a string of dark rubber tires adorning its length like a native necklace. The passage is calm and reflective, the sea air is purifying, and the fog offers welcome cover from all thought and rumination. The island has appeared on the horizon like an immense sea creature, partially submerged, guarding the ocean floor—its humped back and prone neck seemingly lying in wait for just the right moment to pull up its massive back and shake deep-sea raindrops from its immense head.

As the water taxi reaches the pier, Rowley steps out and stops, to a genuflection of coastline and strand. *So this is how they felt: Columbus, Mallory, Heyerdahl, Armstrong.*

But Rowley's journey is neither a small step nor a giant leap. It's an epic vault of consciousness for all those who had lost touch with their soul. He pauses on the pier briefly before striding past campers and hikers, arriving with frame backpacks and adventure duffels, with sleeping bags and bivouac sacks. He follows one of several sandy trails to his posada, where he's greeted with a bottle of coconut water and a map.

This small room would be his base camp—his shelter, his supply depot, and his command post. As he unpacks his computer and phone, he becomes enamored with the sunset. It crowds his small, white-framed window with the henna and fire of the sun's downward journey. It spills across the horizon, brushes the white sands, and touches the heads of old fisherman with a gentle patina of twilight copper and brass.

Time seems neither pertinent nor appropriate here, but Rowley knows that dreams require sleep. He crawls into an overly soft bed with hard sheets and closes his eyes to the smell of brine and the swishing push and pull of rockweed.

The next morning brings song. He awakes to a symphony of tree music from a vibrantly colored orchestra of parakeets and parrots, the fast chirp of the Brazilian tanager, the lyrical whistle of the jungle thrush, the *tap-tap* of the red-tailed woodpecker, and the repetitive low squawk of the spot-billed toucanet.

There are more boats, new groups of surfers and troops of eager explorers, but they fold into the island as naturally as the freshwater marshes, the cattails, and the ground-dwelling pacas. They are here, as he is, to feel nothing and everything—to slip through time and sidestep life, toss their humanity to Earth, dangle their feet in the pools of destiny, drink in the colors of Eden, be grand again in the smaller scheme of things, fall back in love with being, and touch the gentle things of God.

Rowley Gaines has become Henry David Thoreau, who famously went to the woods only to discover that *"[he] had not lived."* He has become W.B. Yeats in a *"bee-loud glade"* on the Lake Isle of Innisfree, and Lord Byron finding *"rapture on the lonely shore."* Rowley is Percy Bysshe Shelley, wandering through the *"dim wilderness of the mind . . . homeless, boundless, and unconfined."* And Robert Frost, who sought to *"get away from earth awhile and then come back to it and begin over."*

Arianna is here. He can feel it. A resonance in the air clings to certain places where she's been, like a haunting perfume. It's draped between the tangled fig trees and the mangroves. It rests in the heavy haze of the broad-leafed rainforests and the shades of the coastal lagoons. Perhaps she's in a cabin at Shell Beach, or reclining in a cove along Passa-Passa, or on the very edge of Nova Brasilia.

He sets out with bottled water, his best *Columbia®* trail shorts, and the only shoes he brought. He leaves his cell phone on the bed, determined to hold this quest solely in his mind. He quickly climbs the long stairs to Farol das Conchas and looks for Arianna from Dom Pedro II's timeless, panoramic overlook. Rowley scrambles Whale Hill, and searches the island's contours and hidden curves. He combs Miguel Beach for her footprints. He enters the cave of *Encantadas,* the Grotto of the Charmed, where mythical women still call men from the sea.

To Rowley, he's a biosphere apart from the trespassers, interlopers, gate-crashers—now brought together by a moment in time, and a window in technology that tosses lifelines to dreams. Arianna is his bridge back home, to the earth, to the sky, to the rapture of mortality, and to the sheer ecstasy of just being alive.

CHAPTER TWELVE

Percy is back at the coffee shop, sitting and waiting on a rare, rainy day in what has been a dry year. When rain comes after a drought, it smells different . . . there's an aura of repudiation, as if the earth has forgotten how to be wet. It stirs the worldly mud around collective things—pavement, handrail, windowpane, swirling storm drains. And one can detect the churning of oils, the thinning of the ozone, and the loosening of the fibers of the ecosphere.

Spontaneous falling water is one of those few, enduring natural phenomena for which we have no recourse—other than to seek cover. When condensation meets gravity, it produces varying degrees of drizzle, showers, downpours, and deluges. It's always raining somewhere on planet Earth and, while it ruins many a parade, it remains one of the grandest atmospheric gestures under which humanity exists.

Percy checks his phone and watches the door. Each time it opens, the smell of wet soles and a damp city blows in, but no one notices. Morgan was right. Everyone bows their heads and bends their necks to their communication devices and their smart phones in an unprecedented display of detachment. The only sound in the café is the gentle pelting of rain on an outside awning, the occasional *beep* of the register, and the thunderous, sporadic blasts of froth.

Margaret Atwood once said, *"Walking into the crowd was like sinking into a stew—you became an ingredient, you took on a certain flavour."* And on this rainy afternoon, each of them takes on the unsavory taste of solitude, as if they'd been simmered, rolled and boiled in a dispassionate soup, now served up in a saltless gumbo in small, forgettable mouthfuls.

Percy ponders how we now find ourselves amidst the glory days of processors, operating systems, encoders, decoders, and native tools—gorged with RAM and faster broadband—yet we've starved our sensibilities. We've plugged into everything and yet unplugged from the planet. The global masses have hooked themselves up to a worldwide tangle of intercommunication and yet disengaged from life.

This progress—this advancement—was never supposed to undo the human race . . . never supposed to dehumanize the population . . . never supposed to paralyze the poetry and the greater dialogue of human life . . . Was it?

They knew they had to get the app back up. They had to turn the story back on. Rowley was, perhaps, the first by-product of the reawakening, proof that the human imagination could indeed be resuscitated.

Morgan rushes in and pulls a dripping hood off her head. Her hair is damp around the edges and her face is wet. She slides into a chair across from Percy.

"I heard from Rowley," Morgan exhales.

Her words resonate across the noiseless, slumping, preoccupied masses.

"Rowley? Did he make it to the island?" Percy raises his brows.

"He did," she smiles.

"And?" he begs, frantically examining her glistening face.

She removes her rain slicker and ceremoniously blots her cheeks dry with a napkin.

"And . . . he says he found her!" she proclaims.

"Not Arianna . . ." Percy's eyes narrow.

"Yes, Arianna . . ." she stares back.

"The woman from the cantina along the I-10 in Indio. California. USA. How is that even possible, Morgan?" he wonders.

"I'm at a loss, too. I don't know how one locates a fabrication dreamed up by hundreds of people from every corner of the earth," she shrugs.

"And a beautiful one at that . . . So what exactly did he say?" he entreats.

Morgan pulls her cell phone from the front pouch of her windbreaker and reads while sweeping her thumb gently up the screen.

"I want you to know that I am well. I am on the island and in the throes of my journey. I have been unshackled. Something about immense desire is highly incarcerating. As soon as I disembarked, I felt emancipated. Albert Camus once said, 'The only way to deal with an unfree world is to become so absolutely free that your very existence is an act of rebellion.'

"I urge everyone to rebel, to celebrate the delirium of not having a plan, to sit in a canopy of jungle trees, to lay thumbprints on things that few have seen.

"I have wandered the island and in no particular direction. On one lonely stretch of Praia Grande, I watched predatory birds feed on a giant, dead sea turtle. They pierced its shell and reached its flesh. Beneath its slow gait and hard outer case was but a soft creature. I am not a poetic man, but surely a metaphor abides there.

"I could not tell if the turtle had been crawling to the sea to die or trying to reach the shore to live. The thing is, we are all on loan from creation and will return one day . . . flat on our back, to some beach at the fringe of a global village by the sea. As we slip our shells and edge toward things we may never reach, our story becomes everything."

Morgan pauses to spy Percy, across the table, completely enthralled. They lock gazes for a moment, and she continues to read Rowley's text.

"I found Arianna in a café by Praia do Farol. She is precisely as they described, right down to 'her dark eyes,' 'broad lips' and 'old-world radiance.' I stood by the door, afraid to advance or retreat, and she smiled—as if knowing everything: Indio, Corinne, Candy . . . Cochabamba, Elena, Beatriz . . . El Alto, Crash, Jake. I was utterly exposed, stripped bare, and felt somewhat ridiculous in my thin, white skin. Somehow, she understood that when a virtual man falls from his cloud, he can never go home. I will tell you more once I have decided upon which beach to crawl, and upon which shore to die.

In friendship and story,
Rowley T. Gaines."

"Morgan, we have to find the guy."

"He's clearly crossed over." she mutters, still staring at the screen. "The question is . . . to where?" her eyes rise to meet Percy's.

"He's on the island with our app and some woman."

"It's not quite 'our' app. We haven't paid for it, Percy. He volunteered, remember?" she says.

"He hijacked our concept, did he not? Isn't that techno-piracy?"

"We don't know what his intentions are," she replies.

"What's up with you? Where's your hunger? What happened to your drive? I thought you wanted to save the English language and revive the art of storytelling? Are you going to just let this thing go?" Percy challenges.

"I just don't want the guy to *off* himself. He sounds unstable," she notes.

"Well, you know what? We can't control what he does. All I know is, if he's found spread-eagle and belly-up next to that turtle, we better already have his passwords!" he blurts.

"So what are you suggesting, Percy? That we chase Rowley Gaines halfway across the world to some remote island? Is that what you're saying?"

"I'm saying that I've never felt so alive as I have over these past few weeks. We've been reconnected with the human spirit. We've brought the entire world to our coffee table. We've passed around a good story, like a good bottle of ripple or a good joint. And all of humanity has taken a sip and a hit and passed it on. For the first time in a long while, I feel like we're going to be okay. I feel like maybe, just maybe, we're going to make it as a civilization. So when future generations look back at this moment in time, they won't speak of it as a period of detached discontent but as a new age of innovation and creative expression.

"We're making that happen, Morgan. We're charting that change for posterity. This is our calling. This is why we've been put here. Pulling all-nighters and running predawn raids to rescue creative expression is our *raison d'être*. So, if it means taking a cut-rate flight to Brazil and jumping on a tired ferry to an island in the South Atlantic to reclaim 'our story,' then that's worth it to me."

Morgan smiles at her longtime friend and drops her head to the table in a gesture of acknowledgment and fatigue. She's tired. Dreams can do that. They can drain one's strength and deplete the reserves of even the most inspired among us. She can't remember exactly when an interactive phone took the place of an inactive relationship, or when an online post replaced a face-to-face "Happy Birthday," or when we could no longer hold the attention of the person sitting across from us—but it had been a while. Morgan thought, how did we get here? We're creatures capable of tremendous vision, and yet few of us can now go a day without being "connected" to some form of portable commotion. Would the world really change all that much if we weren't?

Her grandmother used to say, "Morgan, when I close my eyes at night, the last thing I see is your grandfather's face. I've watched that face unfold next to me in successive chapters . . . from bright beginnings, to rousing interludes, to jarring conflicts, and to lasting conclusions. For fifty years that face has been read and turned, creased and dog-eared, from long days and short nights, tumbled and spilled, from sun-up to sundown—and finally tossed onto a quiet shelf.

"But despite its old cover, we've written a beautiful book together. And sometimes, when the moon is just right, I see that young man with the big smile and the clear eyes put his head down again next to mine, in what seems like a single moment gone by. And I realize that his bedtime whispers have been the conversation of my life."

There was something about her grandmother's immigrant perspective that was vigorously authentic and dynamically real. She savored everything and squandered nothing. Her life was big, and it was immediate. Her greenhorn optimism and keen sense of pragmatism pervaded generations.

Whatever would Grandma think of us now? Morgan wondered.

How would she explain to her a world in which a letter is neither written nor stamped—but captured on a screen and discharged through infinity? How would she describe the billions of messages that are now sent each day, in a Morse code of broken sentences? How would she justify that we now talk more but speak less? How would she defend a virtual book of face-friends, many of whom we've never actually met, or seen, or spoken to?

Her grandmother would say, "You have a strange definition of a friend, Morgan," and Morgan would tell her grandmother that the word itself has surely changed. She would tell her grandmother that so many words have changed.

"Our pillows are empty, Grandma," Morgan whispers. "We look at our phones before closing our eyes. Instead of thanking God for another morning, we look at pictures from someone else's night. We're dying in cars and at railroad crossings, and we're letting robots tell our story."

One would think it would be so much easier now—to compose and combine—to cut and paste one sentiment and move it to a new beginning, or a different ending. There was a time when we would drown in stories. We would bathe in the power of words running recklessly down our backs and through our minds, tangling with memories, colliding with old pictures, conjuring up lost tastes and long-buried scents of summers and winters.

Can this generation's book still be written? Or was it a gross overestimation to believe that the human narrative was powerful enough to silence our vast, modern communication systems? Could personification, metaphor, and hyperbole possibly trump Verizon, T-Mobile, and AT&T?

Morgan looked around the coffee shop. Poor bastards, she thought to herself. They're so much more than just preoccupied; they're downright oppressed. They've been tyrannized and subjugated. They've become as Thoreau said, *"the tools of their tools."* They are as Pasternak described, *"united by the abyss that separated them from the rest of the world."*

She was beginning to see the depth of the crisis and the breadth of the challenge. Percy was right. They had to continue, to push on.

"Thank you, Percy," she finally says, looking up at him from the table. "I'd forgotten why we came this far. Sometimes I need to be poked, prodded, stuffed with paper, and set afire again. Those things that words can do must never be lost, and that's what this is about."

Kafka said, *"What we need are books that hit us like a most painful misfortune, like the death of someone we loved more than ourselves, that make us feel as though we had been banished to the woods, far from any human presence, like a suicide. A book must be the ax for the frozen sea within us."*

It seems fitting, Morgan thought, that her and Percy's journey would now go back to an island where, in so many ways, it all began.

CHAPTER THIRTEEN

It didn't take Morgan and Percy very long to secure a cheap flight to Curitiba, and ferry reservations from Paranaguá to the island. Getting to Ilha do Mel was clearly going to be the easy part. Finding Rowley, on whatever existential parallel he now resided, could prove to be more challenging. And what of Arianna? The irony of Rowley's search for Arianna was not lost on them.

Was Arianna perhaps less a fantasy and more a configuration? Was she a by-product of Rowley's newly reconditioned mind, or one of those materializations that come about when someone wants something so very much, it actually happens? Perhaps she was a girl—any girl on the island—that, by some wrinkle in providence, could be the very woman who owned those black pumps left on the side of the I-10 freeway in Indio, California.

To Rowley, she was a captivating ideal: a maddening, provocative—yet vulnerable—paradigm that forged an unsolvable equation within his computative mind. He'd walked the narrow trails and wooded paths of rational awareness and found all the stories that he had been denied. There was no magnetism in source code, or inherent poetry in an algorithm. There was little music to be found in data transfer. A simple sensor interface brought nothing to mind when he closed his eyes. Arianna, however, brought everything.

She was a creation of collective communication. She was the debutante of a virtual dance. She set Rowley free. As Victor Hugo mused, *"To love or have loved, that is enough. Ask nothing further. There is no other pearl to be found in the dark folds of life."* In the dark folds of Rowley's life, Arianna was an open source and their impossible relationship somehow made software much softer.

When Morgan and Percy arrive in Curitiba, it's raining. They had effectively gone from rain to rain. The ferry to the island is like most transport boats, filled with tourists sprawled across bench seats. They wear caps and herd children. Some cling to rucksacks, while others flip through phrase books, iPhones, and iMaps. An abundance of bright orange life vests are piled overhead in nets. The floors are wet and the seats are damp. The air is filled with the smell of salt and fish, engine fuel and old boat ramps.

Young families move to and fro with babies on their backs. Old couples clutch old books sealed in plastic wrap. A young student takes a selfie in the breeze and an old surfer stands alone with his memories. There is someone from everywhere, a generation for everyone, and a universal exploration of just about everything.

The ocean rolls off the end of the old steel bow like a long gray road toward a grand exile, or to a great escape. Water rushes from the stern as it had some thousand times before. On the horizon line, the island rises in vague mounds, oscillating between loose folds of rain and tight expanses of jungle. Storm clouds seize the marina and etch the harbor's contours from the fog. The sea throws itself against the coast and slaps the massive wave-cut stones before finally rolling across the probing toes of peaceful beachgoers.

Morgan and Percy disembark at the village of Encantadas to a tangle of birds, a tussle of fussy white waves, and astonishingly little man-made noise. One cannot help but notice the absence of human sound. No cars, no planes, no sirens . . . no idling buses, no rumbling jets, no passing trains. They can't decide if it's peaceful or unnerving. It's so quiet, it hurts. They're so devoid of distraction, their brains become boisterous and untamed. Passing thoughts are thunderous, and even the most casual observation is so intense, it is deafening. Their feet move through the white sand with distinct squeaks. Percy's pocket change jingles like a casino cash window, and seabirds swarm overhead, their shrill screams amplified and reverberating.

As they walk toward the village, they stop at one of the first cafés they find and sit in red, plastic chairs under red cloth umbrellas just off the beach. They have a drink called *Caipirinha*—it is perhaps the best drink they'd ever had.

Percy raises his glass. "Well, we made it. I have no idea where we are exactly but it seems very pretty, and I very much love these drinks. Here's to finding Rowley."

Morgan taps his glass, sips her drink, and smiles. "Or the shoes, or the turtle, or Jake and Crash."

"Of course. Any of them would be a critical clue. So where do we begin, captain?" he asks her, while twirling his tiny paper umbrella.

"I'm sitting here thinking, if I were Rowley, where would I go?" she ponders.

"To the Apple Store," Percy replies.

"Of course, and in the absence of that?" she says, still smiling.

"I can't say that I know what techies do on holiday. Do they program things? Do they read Kindles in the shade? Do they run the island's Help Desk?" he asks.

An attentive young waiter brings them two more drinks.

"I don't think Rowley believes he's on holiday. I think he feels this is the journey of his life. His entire existence has been one of tidy answers to concise questions, but now the questions are rambling, and the answers are messy," Morgan conveys.

"Good point. I also think it's the first time that his carefully contrived tchno-architecture has actually spoken back to him," Percy adds.

"Oh, in a mad-creator kind of way?" she asks.

"Is there any other?" he replies.

Morgan sips her drink. "So, is Arianna a kind of e-Frankenstein?" she asks.

"To us, she's been sewn together with spare words, borrowed yarns, and reclaimed anecdotes. But to him, she's a beautiful monster," he points out.

Morgan takes another sip and recites, *"It is true, we shall be monsters, cut off from all the world; but, on that account, we shall be more attached to one another."*

"Morgan Byrnes, are you quoting Mary Shelley?" he asks.

She continues, *"Unhappy man! Do you share my madness? Have you drank also of the intoxicating draught? Hear me—let me reveal my tale, and you will dash the cup from your lips!"*

"Oh, Morgan . . . I could sit here and play with words all day. How many drinks have we had?" he asks.

"Not enough to fix the world, Percy."

"Would you really want to fix it?" he wonders.

"That is so Augustinian of you, sir," she replies.

He finishes his drink and tells her, "I firmly believe that we're not here to fix the world or each other, just to tell the story about how broken everything is."

"We need our app back to do that," she says.

"We do, indeed," he answers.

"So Rowley's text mentions two reference points. The first is a *'lonely stretch of Praia Grande,'* and the second is *'a café by Praia do Farol,'*" she says.

"Okay, and *Praia* means what?" he asks.

"Beach," she answers.

"Of course it does. Why wouldn't it? And on an island with mile upon mile of coastline, how hard can they be to find?"

"Look at the map, it seems all the beaches run together. I think we just need to start walking," she tells him.

"After sitting almost a full day on a plane, a bus, and a boat, a walk across a tropical paradise is fine by me. What more could we ask for, really? Drinks, beaches, beautiful people, and the prospect of finishing our story!" he exclaims.

"A little sunshine would be nice, but I'm not complaining," she responds.

Percy slaps his arm and then the side of his face. "Did the brochure mention mosquitos the size of hummingbirds?" he asks.

"More reason to start moving," Morgan says, as she stands and stretches.

They settle their bill and set out toward the Caminhada Trail, a network of sandy paths, lush grasses, and thick trees that cut across the island and then wind down to the sea. The trails rise and fall and merge with other footpaths. And in the thick of the rain forest, the trees become *"bent in overgrowth,"* as Frost once described.

They come upon several natural, green tunnels. They aren't certain which one Rowley chose, or which may lead to Arianna. They stop to deliberate and, as Frost would say, *"kept the first for another day! Yet knowing how way leads on to way . . . doubted if [they] should ever come back."* They walk alone, they walk together, and sometimes walk with groups of other travelers. Yet each twist and turn seems an exercise in solitude.

As Percy parades through the sand, he thinks about his students. How could he possibly save them from the mediocrity that sets in when people fail to embrace the creative world of observation?

How could he be the teacher they will always remember? How could he train them to articulate a vision of existence that will fill their lives with meaning when they're old men and women? How can he help them see the magnificent dreams that life holds, if their mind's eye is always closed?

For Morgan, the journey is an exercise in enlightenment: *sapere aude*—dare to know. She knows what words do to people. She knows their power and their influence. She understands that language can move us to love and to tears. Words can start wars and flame revolutions. They can bring a grown woman back to her grandmother's kitchen, or a grown man back to his first embrace and kiss. Words can break us up and break us down, and they can absolutely bring us to our knees. They, not the men that speak them, are the masters of history. Kant said, *"We are enriched not by what we possess, but by what we can do without."* As the jungle moves through her, she knows we can never do without words. Despite the road we travel or the company we choose, our journey is a solitary march except for the words and the stories that we share along the way.

Morgan and Percy finally reach the first beach, quietly ensconced in the island's natural contours. There are a handful of strollers and a group of fisherman loading nets into a bright blue boat. The sun has finally broken through the clouds and glitters along the horizon, dancing on the tops of the minibreakers that roll in endless succession toward the shore. The cove is the sea's momentary finale as it spools and lathers onto the quiet strand. Suddenly, it has gotten brighter and warmer.

"Wow, now that's a beach!" Percy exclaims as they emerge from the forest.

"Doesn't it just make you want to live!" she replies, as she runs down across the sand.

"There have been few times in my life, Morgan, that I've felt like I was part of something much larger than myself, and this is clearly one of them," he calls to her.

"This is a love letter to planet Earth, Percy," she shouts back.

"Yours truly, signed *us*," he answers with his arms outstretched.

They continue to walk along curvaceous beaches that expand and contract with the coastline. In some spots, the land meets the sea in a sudden tumble of rocks, followed by a quick retreat into simmering tidal swamps. As the day gets warmer, the sand gets hotter. They move to and from the breakers to rest and cool their feet. Soon the inlets look the same.

The boats and nets become predictable. The same lovers stroll beside the same waves, and the birds have a familiar flock and gait. Nothing is distinguishable; the advancing tides, the collapsing surf, and the slow hiss of vanishing waves. In the blinding delirium of the bright, brazen sun, every man they pass is Rowley, and every woman is Arianna.

Percy stops, and feels his face and eyes. "Morgan, did we bring sunblock by chance?"

"Sorry. No," she answers.

"Thank God for my hat," he says as he pulls his bright red Yosemite cap firmly down above his brows.

"Do you have any water left?" she asks him.

"I was going to ask you," he replies.

They can feel their noses and necks getting hot and sore. Their eyelids feel taut; their lips, dry and parched. Their toes move through the surf like pink crabs burrowing down into the packed sand. Sunburn was setting in, and they were hurting.

Around the next bend, on a distant mound of shoreline, a white beacon suddenly vaults out of the forest. The lighthouse was there to guide ships, to steer lives, and to ignite purpose. A powerful, timeless and brilliant beam of luminosity, it warns of the hazards, dangers and perils that reside here. It seems to sit atop the universe—or at least their part of it—and crowns this leg of their journey, marking the end to this small bit of earth.

Morgan stops and calls back to Percy, "That's *Farol das Conchas* . . . Lighthouse of Shells. According to the map, there are snack bars around here. Let's stop, find some drinks, get some food, and see if someone will sell us sunblock."

"That sounds like a plan I can endorse wholeheartedly," Percy shouts back.

They follow a trail that leads back inland from the beach, and arrive in a lively village of cabins, cottages, lodging houses, and cafés. It smells of grilled meats, hot stews, and spicy barbecues. They can hear jazz and bossa nova. The beat, the strings, the acoustic base, and the sporadic laughter resuscitate their senses.

They slide into high-backed seats under a long, cool awning at a brightly colored fish bar with stout wooden tables, grimacing tiki heads, and large oscillating fans that shuffle the crystal drops on the dangling chandeliers. They gleefully sit down to two plates of oversize shrimp in garlic and oil, with Greek rice, french fries, and several bottles of water. They eat and drink without speaking until they both slowly come back from the brink.

"This is amazing," Percy states with wet lips and oily fingers.

"I will never take food and water for granted again. It's exquisite!" Morgan replies before guzzling half a bottle of water.

"So, I'm wondering if I'm as red as you are." Percy muses.

"How red am I?" she asks.

"Sweetheart, you're a lobster," he admits.

"So are you, my darling," she responds with a smile.

A handsome young waiter comes to the table with more shrimp in a rustic iron pot, a hot bowl of garlic sauce, and more bottles of water. Percy gestures to him, rubbing his arm as if putting on lotion.

"Do you know where we can get sunblock?" He asks in a loud voice while pulling up his shirt sleeve to show his white skin against his newly sunburned skin.

The waiter smiles, nods, leaves briefly, and returns to the table with a bottle of *BullFrog* Sunscreen®, *Surf Formula*.

"Wow. Ask and thou shalt receive!" Percy exclaims. When he attempts to give the waiter money, the young man shakes his head and pushes Percy's hand away.

"Nice kid," Percy comments.

"I wonder where he got the *BullFrog*?" Morgan ponders.

"I bet a tourist left it. Hey . . . maybe it's Rowley's." Percy giggles.

They push their chairs from the table and engage in the unpleasant task of pulling their shirts away from their burnt necks, rolling down their socks, and gingerly applying lotion to their exposed skin.

"This reminds me of being a kid. It was crazy how we fried ourselves. Do you remember trying to shower after a day at the beach?" she asks.

"How can I forget! Toweling off was excruciating!" he exclaims.

"For some reason, we thought being red looked good," she reminisces.

"No, no, no. We wanted the tan that never came, and no matter how many times we burned and peeled, burned and peeled, it just never came!"

They both laugh and drink more water as the young waiter places the bill on the table and begins to clear their plates.

"Wouldn't it be the ultimate irony if Rowley had actually been here?" Morgan ponders. "Sitting at this very table?"

"It would be even more ironic if he was sitting here with Arianna and they both ordered the garlic shrimp," Percy replies.

"So, let's say she's real, Percy. Let's say that she does exist. Wouldn't people know her?" Morgan asks. "I mean, it's not a very big island."

"You would think so, particularly if she's all that, and then some. Let's ask the waiter. He's my new go-to guy. Never hurts to ask," he replies.

Percy taps the waiter on the arm as he carries stacks of dirty dishes. "Excuse me, I'm sorry to bother you again, but do you happen to know who Arianna is? Arianna? She's a beautiful woman? Bella? *Bonito*?" Percy inquires.

The young waiter stops and looks at him. A smile overtakes his face. He gazes into space for several minutes before closing his eyes tightly and then gently nodding his head. "Arianna. *Sim. Eu faço.*"

"You know Arianna?" Percy repeats with disbelief.

"*Sim*," he says, nodding.

"She's a pretty woman with long dark hair and dark eyes. *Bonito*!" Morgan reiterates, while gesturing with her hands.

The young man nods again, "Arianna. *Sim. Sim.*"

When he says her name, it sounds like poetry. His annunciation is low and rolls between his teeth. It's idyllic, like Tennyson's *Maud* or Poe's *Annabel Lee*.

Percy looks at Morgan and then back at the waiter. How enchanting must this woman be? Arianna has lured men across continents and left others utterly speechless. Is this the same girl whose heart was broken by Gustavo inside a Mexican cantina? Could she be the same woman who stepped out of her shoes on the side of the freeway just beyond the desert casino? Could they now be on the brink of finally finding her, locating Rowley, and finishing their story?

"Where is she?" Percy asks in a slow, almost arresting tone. "Where is Arianna?"

"*Ela é ali,*" the waiter says, pointing across the square at a rustic café.

"Over there?" Morgan says, pointing. "Arianna is over there, at Pousada Ilha do Mel?"

He nods and says, "*Em Cyber Café Pousada,*" in an almost melodic declaration.

"Thank you so much," Percy whispers breathlessly.

He takes whatever cash he has in his pocket and puts it in the waiter's hand, cupping it closed to override any objection. He looks at Morgan with a mixture of astonishment, excitement, and dread. "It's a cybercafe!"

"I have a feeling that's very significant," she responds.

They leave the fish bar and move anxiously across the courtyard. The cybercafe is no more than a provincial hut with a small deck enclosed by bamboo screens and casually arranged Adirondack chairs with wicker side tables. A large hammock hangs suspended from a beam near a wooden case filled with books, candles, aperitifs, and exotic bird figurines. As they step onto the porch, the floorboards bend and creak, no doubt from the weight of countless heavy boots and bare feet, from the wear and tear of surfers rushing to and fro, from hikers, lovers, and hopeless believers—and the unwieldy narratives of timeless storytellers.

CHAPTER FOURTEEN

When Morgan and Percy enter the café, it smells of fresh coffee and old paperbacks. Various hand-painted signs encourage customers to TAKE A BOOK AND LEAVE A BOOK in several different languages. It reminds Morgan of a small UK book store where she purchased her very first collection of Shakespeare, or the exotic traveler's library at that bed-and-breakfast in Amsterdam.

There are so many volumes—manuscripts, hardcovers, softcovers—written by so many hands in so many dialects, across countless generations. She wonders what kind of stories the world could tell, and what kind of conversations we could have, if only we would sit down and read again. As Clarence Shepard Day said:

> *"The world of books is the most remarkable creation of man. Nothing else that he builds ever lasts. Monuments fall; nations perish; civilizations grow old and die out; and, after an era of darkness, new races build others. But in the world of books are volumes that have seen this happen again and again, and yet live on, still young, still as fresh as the day they were written, still telling men's hearts of the hearts of men centuries dead."*

There, in a room of books, at long last, they have found Rowley—seated on the floor of *Em Cyber Café Pousada*, the Cyber

Café. He looks different, somewhat changed. If a man could carry the expression of enlightenment, then this would describe his face. His skin is awash in wakefulness, his jaw firm and fixed, his eyes penetrating, his breaths deep and slow—as if every exhalation pulls meaning from his bones. He is now a man engaged in an epic and heroic dialogue with existence.

It doesn't take long to identify Arianna. She's seated in a large wooden chair, as if preparing to give a talk or a reading. The infamous Prada pumps are on a small table beside her. Rowley watches her every gesture and movement. He observes her, adoringly, much as Gabriel García Márquez looked upon Fermina Daza.

> *"To him, she seemed so beautiful, so seductive, so different from ordinary people, that he could not understand why no one was as disturbed as he by the clicking of her heels on the paving stones, why no one else's heart was wild with the breeze stirred by the sighs of her veils, why everyone did not go mad with the movements of her braid, the flight of her hands, the gold of her laughter. He had not missed a single one of her gestures, not one of the indications of her character, but he did not dare approach her for fear of destroying the spell."*

Other young men arrive and also take a spot on the floor in the rustic island café. A man with close-cropped hair resembles Crash, and another with blonder, more tousled hair, could very well be Jake Waring. In a gathering of posterities, each is equally aroused by Arianna's life force. They look up, not down. There are no phones or headsets, no laptops or tablets. There are only words and reflections, and the keenness of the very mindful things that connect people.

Morgan and Percy watch the scene with silent fascination.

Percy leans into Morgan and puts his lips right up to her ear. "She's . . . She's . . . absolutely decrepit," he states with amazement.

Morgan surveys the room. "No, Percy. You're wrong. She's breathtaking."

Arianna is in fact very old. She's perhaps the oldest person they've ever seen, but she's not here to be young. She is here to be heard. Her long, white hair frames a small, withered face. Her cheeks are cavernous. Her skin is weathered and windswept—much like the island, it has been eroded by the relentless seasons of life. Her dark, native eyes sit in tight folds, tucked between the creases of time.

Her ears are oversized, her feet broad and fossilized—and her hands . . . dark, leathery, and fibrous. She wears a single black ribbon in her hair. A trio of silver bracelets dangle from her lean arms and turquoise rings orbit her long, dark fingers.

When her thin lips finally speak, the café patrons stop, the island settles, the tide abates—the entire peninsula comes to a poetic pause. Arianna is a storyteller and the island is her metaphor for unattained dreams. Eudora Welty once said:

> *"It had been startling and disappointing to me to find out that storybooks had been written by people, that books were not natural wonders, coming up of themselves like grass. Yet regardless of where they come from, I cannot remember a time when I was not in love with them—with the books themselves, cover and binding and the paper they were printed on, with their smell and their weight and with their possession in my arms, captured and carried off to myself."*

As Arianna speaks, her bracelets rattle and her rings rap against the curve of the armchair. She talks in symbols and speaks in dreams, particularly to those who have spent a lifetime waiting for destiny.

"On the island," she says, "destiny arrives with the weather. There is always sunrise and sunset. The shore is always coming. The tide is always going, and our words are the oars that launch us off to sea and bring us home again."

Rowley sighs and smiles. He has clearly found context. He is no longer on the edges of life looking in. Suddenly, his theories of computation, his processes of automation—all the virtual environments of his life—have purpose. He's a participant.

For his part, Percy seizes the poetry in the day's events. "We should all have an Arianna and a hammock at *Pousada Ilha do Mel* to hang between heaven and reality," he muses. "We should all have lives that never fall between the floorboards of island porches. We should all have special places where a thousand voices can band together to tell a single magnificent story."

Morgan knows that Arianna has always been. She recognizes her. She's the *Old Woman of the Roads* and the *Old Woman of Beare*. She's the soothsayer and the siren, the femme fatale and the temptress, the banshee and the storyteller. As she speaks, Morgan returns to those long-ago summers, listening once again to the *tap, tap, tap* of her mother's typewriter and the *beep, beep, beep* of her Smith Corona word processor . . . the endless shifting of her dot matrix printer and all the dialogues of her life.

It seems fitting that it would end here, on an island within an ecosystem that has thrived for centuries within a community of organisms. Now without noise or paper, pen or tablet, ink or keystroke, screen or processor—humanity could bring its experiences back together again.

At that moment, a loud intermittent clinking and blinking rouses Morgan. It's alternating, mechanical, and sporadic. It's shrill, discordant, and extraneous. She's not in the coffee shop . . . she's not on the island. She's in the car with Percy, and they've just pulled off the freeway. He's turning left down a side street.

Percy shifts his eyes from the road. "Are you awake? I lost you just after Monterey. You've been on quite the trip my friend—talking, walking, quoting, and reciting. You feeling all right? Let me look at you."

Morgan turns and looks at him through the fast-passing reflections of urban scramble; the rapid fire of glass and walls, wire and poles, hordes of cars, clusters of noise—the ebb and flow of life back home.

"Jeez. You look like Dorothy after the window frame hit her in the head!" Percy exclaims.

"I feel like her, too," she mumbles meekly.

"So, are we going to sell out to the Silicons or try to build this app all on our own?" he asks.

Morgan takes a sip from a water bottle that had been loosely cradled in her hand and smiles. "I'm not much for selling out, Percy. And besides . . . I think we already have our first story."

BIBLIOGRAPHY OF EXCERPTS:

[The eBook version of The Island contains live reference links per attribution, for the convenience of the curious reader.]

Page 1:

Her diplomas are carefully framed on a long wall with a copy of My Creed by Dean Alfange, which hung in her father's office throughout her childhood. She particularly loves this part:

> *"It is my right to be uncommon—if I can. I seek opportunity—not security. I do not wish to be a kept citizen, humbled and dulled by having the state look after me. I want to take the calculated risk; to dream and to build, to fail and to succeed."*

ATTRIBUTION: **"My Creed"** by Dean Alfange, *This Week Magazine* and *The Reader's Digest,* (October 1952)

> *I do not choose to be a common man.* **It is my right to be uncommon—if I can. I seek opportunity—not security. I do not wish to be a kept citizen, humbled and dulled by having the state look after me. I want to take the calculated risk; to dream and to build, to fail and to succeed.** *I refuse to barter incentive for a dole. I prefer the challenges of life to the guaranteed existence; the thrill of fulfillment to the stale calm of utopia. I will not trade freedom for beneficence nor my dignity for a handout. I will never cower before*

141

any master nor bend to any threat. It is my heritage to stand erect, proud and unafraid; to think and act for myself, enjoy the benefit of my creations, and to face the world boldly and say, this I have done. All this is what it means to be an American.

Page 21:

She'll try to tell them that stories are really what connect us and that every techno-pathway they create is only as good as the message it carries. The narrative has been the single unifying force of human civilization, giving us context and critical meaning. But *"the falcon cannot hear the falconer."* Leave it to Yeats to perfectly describe our monumental disconnect.

ATTRIBUTION: *The Second Coming*, by William Butler Yeats. From *The Collected Poems of W.B. Yeats* (1989); Verse 1:

Turning and turning in the widening gyre
The falcon cannot hear the falconer;
Things fall apart; the centre cannot hold;
Mere anarchy is loosed upon the world,
The blood-dimmed tide is loosed, and everywhere
The ceremony of innocence is drowned;
The best lack all conviction, while the worst
Are full of passionate intensity.

Page 30:

"Rudyard Kipling once said, '*If history were taught in the form of stories, it would never be forgotten,*'" she answers . . ."Let me be more direct. People love to tell stories, and the digital age is robbing us of oral tradition. We've forgotten how to express ourselves with full thoughts and whole words—and if we don't make a change, we'll be the first civilization incapable of conveying its own narrative…"

ATTRIBUTION: Rikki-Tikki-Tavi: *The Jungle Book*, by Rudyard Kipling (1894)

Page 34:

"*What a piece of work is a man! How noble in reason! How infinite in faculty!*" said Hamlet. Man is a piece of work alright! And our reason and faculty have rationalized us into twenty-first-century brutes, once again communicating in crude symbols. Perhaps hundreds of years from now in some buried room, the people of the future will find and "unfinished" text message and marvel at how very ineloquent we were.

ATTRIBUTION: *Hamlet*, by William Shakespeare (1603); *Prince of Denmark*; Act II; Scene II, 250.

Ham. I will tell you why; so shall my anticipation prevent your discovery, and your secrecy to the king and queen moult no feather. I have of late,—but wherefore I know not,—lost all my mirth, forgone all custom of exercises; and indeed it goes so heavily with my disposition that this goodly frame, the earth, seems to me a sterile promontory; this most excellent canopy, the air, look you, this brave o'erhanging firmament, this majestical roof fretted with golden fire, why, it appears no other thing to me but a foul and pestilent congregation of vapours. *What a piece of work is a man! How noble in reason! how infinite in faculty!* in form, in moving, how express and admirable! in action how like an angel! in apprehension how like a god! the beauty of the world! the paragon of animals! And yet, to me, what is this quintessence of dust? man delights not me; no, nor woman neither, though, by your smiling, you seem to say so.

Page 34:

Aristotle once said, "*When the storytelling goes bad in society, the result is decadence.*" . . . Today, the speed of technology has led to a type of linguistic debauchery where we now advocate acronyms, abbreviations, and broken speech. It's all about brevity and limitation. It's about speed and ease. In the process, our intellectual standards have dissipated into a cyber gumbo that lacks consistency, creativity, or composition.

ATTRIBUTION: *Poetics*, by Aristotle (335 BC); as quoted in Robert McKee's "Story – Substance, Structure, Style and the Principles of Screenwriting." [page 13]

Page 35:

"*Fill your paper with the breathings of your heart,*" said Wordsworth.

What William didn't know was that paper would one day be gone, superseded by a liquid crystal display that would hold all the ramblings of a simulated world. The real tragedy would rest with the human heart, which has been beating for centuries, only to now languish somewhere in short-lived, electronic chirps.

ATTRIBUTION: *Letter to his Wife*, William Wordsworth (1812); p. 112

"*Write to me frequently and the longest letters possible; never mind whether you have facts or no to communicate; **fill your paper with the breathings of your heart.***
Most tenderly, your friend and Husband
W.W.

Page 35:

Our only hope and saving grace is to rally those raconteurs among us to continue to tell our fascinating human tale. Perhaps Victor Hugo had it right when he said, "***A writer is a world trapped inside a person.***" It is, after all, a calling. Writers are the mirrors of our time, with something so pressing to say that their only relief is to write it down. So this, then, is a call to arms. A grand charge. A mobilization!

ATTRIBUTION: Victor Hugo (1802-1885); From *La Légende des Siecles (Legend of the Centuries)* 1859, Nouvelle Series XX: Un Poete est Un Monde. Translated to English from "Un poete est un mode enferme dans un homme."

Page 35:

"You can't stay in your corner of the forest waiting for others to come to you. You have to go to them sometimes." Alas, Winnie the Pooh understood the urgency of going to them. He was forever going to and fro, looking for snacks and meaningful conversation with Owl, Piglet, or Rabbit…How would we acknowledge and preserve Hamlet and Aristotle, Wordsworth and Hugo—and Pooh? Would this app be the way? Were these three men before Morgan her Owl, Piglet and Rabbit? Were they there to help her find meaningful conversation?

ATTRIBUTION: *Winnie-the-Pooh*, by A. A. Milnes (1926)

Page 40:

What if it goes viral? What if it doesn't? If they opt not to build her app, she's already decided she'll go back to the "greasers" as Billy Joel once declared, to continue her life as a corporate writer. It was a painstakingly anonymous and comfortably numb existence. Pink Floyd's refrain starts up in her head:

When I was a child
I caught a fleeting glimpse
Out of the corner of my eye.
I turned to look, but it was gone.
I cannot put my finger on it now.
The child is grown.
The dream is gone.
I have become comfortably numb.

ATTRIBUTION: *Comfortably Numb*, from the album *The Wall*, by Pink Floyd (June 23, 1980)

Page 52:

He looks at her and says, "'*The struggle itself towards the heights is enough to fill a man's heart.*' Like Camus, my heart is full, at least until we push our rock to the top of the mountain."

ATTRIBUTION: *The Myth of Sisyphus and Other Essays,* by Albert Camus (1942)

I leave Sisyphus at the foot of the mountain! One always finds one's burden again. But Sisyphus teaches the higher fidelity that negates the gods and raises rocks. He too concludes that all is well. This universe henceforth without a master seems to him neither sterile nor futile. Each atom of that stone, each mineral flake of that night filled mountain, in itself forms a world. The struggle itself toward the heights is enough to fill a man's heart. One must imagine Sisyphus happy.

Page 54:

Without stories, there's no comedy or tragedy, no history or allegory, no success or failure, no truth or fiction, and—above all—no miracles, about which C. S. Lewis once said, "*. . . miracles . . . are a retelling in small letters of the very same story which is written across the whole world in letters too large for some of us to see.*"

ATTRIBUTION: *God in the Dock: Essays on Theology and Ethics*, by C.S. Lewis (1972); p. 29

"*The miracles in fact are a retelling in small letters of the very same story which is written across the whole world in letters too large for some of us to see. Of that larger script part is already visible, part still unsolved. In other words, some of the miracles do locally what God has already done universally: other do locally what He has not yet done, but will do. In that sense, and from our human point of view, some are reminders and other prophesies.*"

Page 54:

The visionary mind is so much larger than that. It's the perfect witness to the human condition and the wild diversity of existence. Louis MacNeice called it, "*The drunkenness of things being various,*" which aptly describes the pleasing intoxication of raw experience. It's that euphoria that has allowed the narrative to survive.

ATTRIBUTION: *Snow*, by Louis MacNeice (1935); Verse 2

World is crazier and more of it than we think,
Incorrigibly plural. I peel and portion
A tangerine and spit the pips and feel
The drunkenness of things being various.

Page 60:

Shakespeare was clear about the imperfection of mankind and the distinctly human tendency to blame our indiscretions on supreme external forces, as illustrated by Edmund, the illegitimate son of the Earl of Gloucester, in King Lear.

This is the excellent foppery of the world, that, when we are sick in fortune, often the surfeit of our own [behavior], we make guilty of our disasters the sun, the moon, and the stars; as if we were villains [of] necessity; fools by heavenly compulsion; knaves, thieves, and treachers by spherical predominance; drunkards, liars, and adulterers by an enforc'd obedience of planetary influence; and all that we are evil in, by a divine thrusting on.

ATTRIBUTION: *King Lear*, by William Shakespeare (1606); from Scene II, The Earl of Gloucester's castle.

Page 60:

Dylan Thomas implored us to reject death; to be rough, wild, and thundering at the end of our days, so we have no regrets—particularly as to our failure to "fork lightning," or to tell our unique tale.

> *Do not go gentle into that good night,*
> *Old age should burn and rave at close of day;*
> *Rage, rage against the dying of the light.*
> *Though wise men at their end know dark is right,*
> *Because their words had forked no lightning, they*
> *Do not go gentle into that good night.*

ATTRIBUTION: "Do not go gentle into that good night," from *In Country Sleep, and other Poems,* by Dylan Thomas (1952)

Page 61:

In *Moby-Dick,* Herman Melville praised the individual merits of the whale. Scholars have argued for generations about whether the beast represents power and independence, or evil and malevolence. It may, in fact, be all those things, since the creature brings out all the persistence and resolve of the human spirit, as well as the weaknesses and the limitations of the human condition.

It does seem to me, that herein we see the rare virtue of a strong individual vitality, and the rare virtue of thick walls, and the rare virtue of interior spaciousness. Oh, man! Admire and model thyself after the whale! Do thou, too, remain warm among ice. Do thou, too, live in this world without being of it. Be cool at the equator; keep thy blood fluid at the Pole. Like the great dome of [Saint] Peter's, and like the great whale, retain, O man! in all seasons a temperature of thine own.

ATTRIBUTION: *Moby-Dick; or, The Whale*, by Herman Melville (1851)

Page 84:

"Someone once said, '*I am enough of an artist to draw freely upon my imagination. Imagination is more important than knowledge. Knowledge is limited. Imagination encircles the world.*' Do you know who said that, Rowley? Do you?" Morgan asks.

ATTRIBUTION: Albert Einstein, in "*What Life Means to Einstein, An Interview by George Sylvester Viereck,*" *The Saturday Evening Post* (1929), p. 117

Page 88:

Cedric used to quote Dostoyevsky, who said, "*The mystery of human existence lies not in just staying alive but in finding something to live for.*" Cedric lived for Beatriz. He was a simple man, and a very good man.

ATTRIBUTION: *The Brothers Karamazov*, by Fyodor Dostoyevsky (1880)

"For the mystery of human existence lies not in just staying alive, but in finding something to live for. Without a concrete idea of what he is living for, man would refuse to live, would rather exterminate himself than remain on earth, even though everywhere around him was bread."

Page 107:

It was precisely as Morgan has always believed—that art was possible in every man. That stories exist in every heart. As the painter, Robert Henri, said:

When the artist is alive in any person, whatever his kind of work may be, he becomes an inventive, searching, daring, self-expressive creature. He becomes interesting to other people. He disturbs, upsets, enlightens, and opens ways for better understanding. Where those who are not artists are trying to close the book, he opens it and shows there are still more pages possible.

ATTRIBUTION: *The Art Spirit*, by Robert Henri (1929)

Page 107:

He knew that life was about chance and that love was about desire. As Nietzsche said, ". . . *the voice of beauty speaks softly; it creeps only into the most awakened souls.*" And, so, Rowley's soul had finally been awakened, and his story was, in many ways, just beginning.

ATTRIBUTION: *Thus Spoke Zarathustra*, by Friedrich Nietzsche (1883)

"But the voice of beauty speaks softly; it creeps only into the most awakened souls. Softly today my shield trembled and laughed; it is the holy laughter and trembling of beauty. At you, virtuous ones, my beauty laughed today."

Page 108:

They knew they had to endorse his journey. They simply could not lobby for a return to creative expression and yet deny Rowley his creative fantasy. They couldn't question his devotion to Arianna, wherever—or however—she exists to him. D.H. Lawrence perhaps explained it best:

No form of love is wrong, so long as it is love, and you yourself honour what you are doing. Love has an extraordinary variety of forms! And that is all there is in life, it seems to me. But I grant you, if you deny the variety of love, you deny love altogether. If you try to specialize love into one set of accepted feelings, you wound the very soul of love. Love must be multi-form, else it is just tyranny, just death.

ATTRIBUTION: *The Ladybird*, by D.H. Lawrence (1921)

*'Well, do you know,' said the Major, 'it seems to me there is really only one supreme contact, the contact of love. Mind you, the love may take on an infinite variety of forms. And in my opinion, **no form of love is wrong, so long as it is love, and you yourself honour what you are doing. Love has an extraordinary variety of forms! And that is all that there is in life, it seems to me. But I grant you, if you deny the variety of love you deny love altogether. If you try to specialize love into one set of accepted feelings, you wound the very soul of love. Love must be multi-form, else it is just tyranny, just death.'***

Pages 110-111:

Rowley Gaines has become Henry David Thoreau, who famously went to the woods only to discover that "*[he] had not lived¹.*" He has become W.B. Yeats in a "*bee-loud glade²*" on the Lake Isle of Innisfree, and Lord Byron finding "*rapture on the lonely shore³.*" Rowley is Percy Bysshe Shelley, wandering through the "*dim wilderness of the mind . . . homeless, boundless, and unconfined⁴.*" And Robert Frost, who sought to "*get away from earth awhile and then come back to it and begin over⁵.*"

ATTRIBUTIONS:

1 *Walden, or Life in the Woods*, by Henry David Thoreau (1854)

"*I went to the woods because I wished to live deliberately, to front only the essential facts of life, and see if I could not learn what it had to teach, and not, when I came to die, **discover that I had not lived.** I did not wish to live what was not life, living is so dear; nor did I wish to practise resignation, unless it was quite necessary. I wanted to live deep and suck out all the marrow of life, to live so sturdily and Spartan-like as to put to rout all that was not life, to cut a broad swath and shave close, to drive life into a corner, and reduce it to its lowest terms.*"

2 *The Lake Isle of Innisfree*, by William Butler Yeats (1865); Verse 1

I WILL arise and go now, and go to Innisfree,
And a small cabin build there, of clay and wattles made;
Nine bean rows will I have there, a hive for the honey bee,
*And live alone in the **bee-loud glade**.*

3 *Childe Harold's Pilgrimage*, by George Gordon Byron (1812)

"*There is a pleasure in the pathless woods,*
*There is a **rapture on the lonely shore**,*
There is society, where none intrudes,
By the deep Sea, and music in its roar:
I love not Man the less, but Nature more,
From these our interviews, in which I steal

From all I may be, or have been before,
To mingle with the Universe, and feel
What I can ne'er express, yet cannot all conceal."

4 ***Fragment: A Wanderer, Poetical Works***, by Percy Bysshe
Shelley (1839)

He wanders, like a day-appearing dream,
*Through the **dim wildernesses of the mind;***
Through desert woods and tracts, which seem
*Like ocean, **homeless, boundless, unconfined.***

5 ***"Birches," Mountain Interval***, by Robert Frost (1916)

*"I'd like to **get away from earth awhile***
And then come back to it and begin over.
May no fate wilfully misunderstand me
And half grant what I wish and snatch me away
Not to return. Earth's the right place for love:
I don't know where it's likely to go better."

Page 114

Margaret Atwood once said, "***Walking into the crowd was***
like sinking into a stew—you became an ingredient, you took on a
certain flavour." And on this rainy afternoon, each of them takes
on the unsavory taste of solitude, as if they'd been simmered, rolled
and boiled in a dispassionate soup, now served up in a saltless
gumbo in small, forgettable mouthfuls.

ATTRIBUTION: *The Blind Assassin*, by Margaret Atwood (2000)

Page 115:

"Albert Camus once said, *'The only way to deal with an unfree world is to become so absolutely free that your very existence is an act of rebellion.'*

"I urge everyone to rebel, to celebrate the delirium of not having a plan, to sit in a canopy of jungle trees, to lay thumbprints on things that few have seen..."

ATTRIBUTION: *The Outsider*, by Albert Camus (1942)

Page 120:

Morgan looked around the coffee shop. Poor bastards, she thought to herself. They're so much more than just preoccupied; they're downright oppressed. They've been tyrannized and subjugated. They've become as Thoreau said, "**the tools of their tools[1].**" They are as Pasternak described, "**united by the abyss that separated them from the rest of the world[2].**"

ATTRIBUTIONS:

1 *Walden, or Life in the Woods*, by Henry David Thoreau (1854); Chapter 1, Economy, Paragraph 15

*The very simplicity and nakedness of man's life in the primitive ages imply this advantage, at least, that they left him still but a sojourner in nature. When he was refreshed with food and sleep, he contemplated his journey again. He dwelt, as it were, in a tent in this world, and was either threading the valleys, or crossing the plains, or climbing the mountain-tops. **But lo! men have become the tools of their tools.** The man who independently plucked the fruits when he was hungry is become a farmer; and he who stood under a tree for shelter, a housekeeper. We now no longer camp as for a night, but have settled down on earth and forgotten heaven.*

2 ***Doctor Zhivago***, by Boris Pasternak (1957)

*"Still more than by the communion of souls, they were **united by the abyss that separated them from the rest of the world.**"*

Page 120:

". . . I'd forgotten why we came this far. Sometimes I need to be poked, prodded, stuffed with paper, and set afire again. Those things that words can do must never be lost, and that's what this is about."

Kafka said, *"What we need are books that hit us like a most painful misfortune, like the death of someone we loved more than ourselves, that make us feel as though we had been banished to the woods, far from any human presence, like a suicide. A book must be the ax for the frozen sea within us."*

ATTRIBUTION: Franz Kafka, in a letter to Oskar Pollak (1904)

Altogether, I think we ought to read only books that bite and sting us. If the book does not shake us awake like a blow to the skull, why bother reading it in the first place? So that it can make us happy, as you put it? Good God, we'd be just as happy if we had no books at all; books that make us happy we could, in a pinch, also write ourselves. **What we need are books that hit us like a most painful misfortune, like the death of someone we loved more than ourselves, that make us feel as though we had been banished to the woods, far from any human presence, like a suicide. A book must be the ax for the frozen sea within us.** *That is what I believe.*

Page 122:

She was a creation of collective communication. She was the debutante of a virtual dance. She set Rowley free. As Victor Hugo mused, "**To love or have loved, that is enough. Ask nothing further. There is no other pearl to be found in the dark folds of life.**"

ATTRIBUTION: *Les Misérables*, by Victor Hugo (1862)

Page 124:

Morgan sips her drink. "So, is Arianna a kind of e-Frankenstein?" she asks.

"To us, she's been sewn together with spare words, borrowed yarns, and reclaimed anecdotes. But to him, she's a beautiful monster," he points out.

Morgan takes another sip and recites, "*'It is true, we shall be monsters, cut off from all the world; but, on that account, we shall be more attached to one another[1].'*"

"Morgan Byrnes, are you quoting Mary Shelley?" he asks.

She continues, "*'Unhappy man! Do you share my madness? Have you drank also of the intoxicating draught? Hear me—let me reveal my tale, and you will dash the cup from your lips![2]'*"

ATTRIBUTION: *Frankenstein*, by Mary Shelley (1818)

1 *"I intended to reason. This passion is detrimental to me, for you do not reflect that you are the cause of its excess. If any being felt emotions of benevolence towards me, I should return them a hundred and a hundredfold; for that one creature's sake I would make peace with the whole kind! But I now indulge in dreams of bliss that cannot be realized. What I ask of you is reasonable and moderate; I demand a creature of another sex, but as hideous as myself; the gratification is small, but it is all that I can receive, and it shall content me. **It is true, we shall be monsters, cut off from all the world; but on that account we shall be more attached to one another.** Our lives will not be happy, but they will be harmless and free from the misery I now feel. Oh! My creator, make me happy; let me feel gratitude towards you for one benefit! Let me see that I excite the sympathy of some existing thing; do not deny me my request!"*

2 At first I perceived that he tried to suppress his emotion; he placed his hands before his eyes; and my voice quivered and failed me, as I beheld tears trickle fast from between his fingers -- a groan burst from his heaving breast. I paused; -- at length he spoke, in broken accents: -- "Unhappy man! Do you share my madness? Have you drank also of the intoxicating draught? Hear me -- let me reveal my tale, and you will dash the cup from your lips!"

Page 125:

They came upon several natural, green tunnels. They aren't certain which one Rowley chose, or which may lead to Arianna. They stop to deliberate and, as Frost would say, *"kept the first for another day! Yet knowing how way leads on to way . . . doubted if [they] should ever come back."*

ATTRIBUTION: *The Road Not Taken; Mountain Interval*, by Robert Frost (1916); Verse 3

And both that morning equally lay
In leaves no step had trodden black.
Oh, I kept the first for another day!
Yet knowing how way leads on to way,
I doubted if I should ever come back.

Page 126:

Words can break us up and break us down, and they can absolutely bring us to our knees. They, not the men that speak them, are the masters of history. Kant said, *"We are enriched not by what we possess, but by what we can do without."* As the jungle moves through her, she knows we can never do without words. Despite the road we travel or the company we choose, our journey is a solitary march except for the words and the stories that we share along the way.

ATTRIBUTION: *Critique of Pure Reason, Second Edition,* by Immanuel Kant (1787); *The Critique of Pure Reason* (German: Kritik der reinen Vernunft) by Immanuel Kant, first published in 1781, second edition 1787.

"We are not rich by what we possess but by what we can do without."

Page 133:

There are so many volumes—manuscripts, hardcovers, softcovers—written by so many hands in so many dialects, across countless generations. She wonders what kind of stories the world could tell, and what kind of conversations we could have, if only we would sit down and read again. As Clarence Shepard Day said:

"The world of books is the most remarkable creation of man. Nothing else that he builds ever lasts. Monuments fall; nations

perish; civilizations grow old and die out; and, after an era of darkness, new races build others. But in the world of books are volumes that have seen this happen again and again, and yet live on, still young, still as fresh as the day they were written, still telling men's hearts of the hearts of men centuries dead."

ATTRIBUTION: *The Story of the Yale University Press Told by a Friend,* by Clarence Day, pp. 7-8 (1920)

Page 134:

He observes her, adoringly, much as Gabriel García Márquez looked upon Fermina Daza.

"To him, she seemed so beautiful, so seductive, so different from ordinary people, that he could not understand why no one was as disturbed as he by the clicking of her heels on the paving stones, why no one else's heart was wild with the breeze stirred by the sighs of her veils, why everyone did not go mad with the movements of her braid, the flight of her hands, the gold of her laughter. He had not missed a single one of her gestures, not one of the indications of her character, but he did not dare approach her for fear of destroying the spell."

ATTRIBUTION: *Love in the Time of Cholera,* by Gabriel García Márquez

Page 135:

When her thin lips finally speak, the café patrons stop, the island settles, the tide abates—the entire peninsula comes to a poetic pause. Arianna is a storyteller, and the island is her metaphor for unattained dreams. Eudora Welty once said:

"It had been startling and disappointing to me to find out that storybooks had been written by people, that books were not natural wonders, coming up of themselves like grass. Yet regardless of where they come from, I cannot remember a time when I was not in love with them—with the books themselves, cover and binding and the paper they were printed on, with their smell and their weight and with their possession in my arms, captured and carried off to myself."

ATTRIBUTION: *One Writer's Beginnings*, by Eudora Welty (1983)

Page 136:

Morgan knows that Arianna has always been. She recognizes her. She's the **Old Woman of the Roads**[1] and the **Old Woman of Beare**[2]. She's the soothsayer and the siren, the femme fatale and the temptress, the banshee and the storyteller. As she speaks, Morgan returns to those long-ago summers, listening once again to the *tap, tap, tap* of her mother's typewriter and the *beep, beep, beep* of her Smith Corona word processor . . . the endless shifting of her dot matrix printer and all the dialogues of her life.

ATTRIBUTIONS:

1 *An Old Woman of the Roads*, by Padraic Colum (1881)

O, TO have a little house!
To own the hearth and stool and all!
The heaped up sods upon the fire,
The pile of turf against the wall!
To have a clock with weights and chains   5
And pendulum swinging up and down!
A dresser filled with shining delph,
Speckled and white and blue and brown!
I could be busy all the day
Clearing and sweeping hearth and floor,   10
And fixing on their shelf again
My white and blue and speckled store!
I could be quiet there at night
Beside the fire and by myself,
Sure of a bed and loth to leave   15
The ticking clock and the shining delph!
Och! but I'm weary of mist and dark,
And roads where there's never a house nor bush,
And tired I am of bog and road,
And the crying wind and the lonesome hush!   20
And I am praying to God on high,
And I am praying Him night and day,
For a little house—a house of my own—
Out of the wind's and the rain's way.

2 *The Lament of the Old Woman of Beare*, *Anonymous, 9th Century, Irish Gallic Poetry*

www.gutenberg.org says:

"The reason why she was called the Old Woman of Beare was that she had fifty foster-children in Beare. She had seven periods of youth one after another, so that every man who had lived with her came to die of old age, and her grandsons and great-grandsons were tribes and races. For a hundred years she wore the veil which Cummin had blessed upon her head. Thereupon old age and infirmity came to her. 'Tis then she said:

> Ebb-tide to me as of the sea!
> Old age causes me reproach.
> Though I may grieve thereat—
> Happiness comes out of fat.
> I am the Old Woman of Beare,
> An ever-new smock I used to wear:
> To-day—such is my mean estate—
> I wear not even a cast-off smock…

TRADEMARK ATTRIBUTIONS:

Smith Corona™ is a registered trademark of Smith Corona Corporation.

Wite-Out® is a registered trademarkk of BIC Group.

Liquid Paper® is a registered trademark of Newell Rubbermaid.

MapQuest is a free online mapping service owned by America Online, Inc.

QT was a product of Coppertone. Coppertone® is a registered trademark of Bayer.

Starbucks™ is a registered trademark of Starbucks Corporation.

Coke™ is a registered trademark of the Coca-Cola Company.

iPhone®, iPad®, iMac® and MacBook Air® are registered trademarks of Apple Inc.

PowerPoint is developed by Microsoft Corporation.

5-hour ENERGY® is a registered trademark of Living Essentials LLC.

Call of Duty® is a trademark of Activision Publishing, Inc. All rights reserved.

A NOTE ABOUT THE AUTHOR

Patricia Mahon is an award-winning poet, screenwriter, playwright, and a former teaching fellow and writing instructor at several major universities, including Tulane and the University of Denver. A native of New York with dual Irish/American citizenship, Mahon is a graduate of Manhattanville College, a W.B. Yeats scholar, having studied under A.S. Knowland, in Oxford, England, and a holder of advanced degrees in Anglo-Irish Literature from Trinity College in Dublin, Ireland. Mahon has also penned several musicals and original songs. Volume 3 of her Age of Distraction series, *The Abbey* (Balcony 7, 2017) is based on her three-act stage play, *The Abbey Yard*, produced in Los Angeles in 2000 with a six-week run. She resides in Los Angeles, California.

Follow Patricia Mahon and *The Age of Distraction* series on social media, www.theageofdistraction.com, and www.balcony7. com

MORE STORIES FROM THE AGE OF DISTRACTION

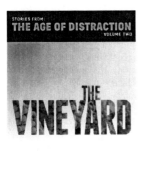

Volume Two: The Vineyard

Morgan and Percy's app has gained global attention but despite thousands of downloads, the world remains inattentive and unfocused. They decide they must go directly to the source of the human narrative, and set out to find the world's greatest living storytellers who like Arianna, have the hypnotic ability to captivate and engage. They hear about a man named Bartholomew Bishop, an agriculturalist, a vintner, and a grape whisperer who summons primordial voices from the soil and instills them into the vines, fruit and skins of his most "complex" wines. It is said that Bartholomew cultivates the stories of mankind. Their search for him takes them to California Wine Country and on a rainy night in Olive Tree Canyon, with no road home, no electricity or cellular service, they pass the night drinking pinot with distracted strangers who tell the stories of their lives for the very first time. **September 2016**

MORE STORIES FROM THE AGE OF DISTRACTION

Volume Three: The Abbey

Morgan traces one of her family's most celebrated stories. She returns to Ireland to walk through the small town where her grandmother was a girl. It is there in the Village of the Monks, at the perimeter of an ancient Abbey that Sadie Connelly encountered a man that would occupy her life. John Holden was her father, but also a casualty of ignorance, hate, bigotry and war. The Duiske Abbey is an enduring tribute to high monasticism, but also the site of unspeakable violence. Her grandmother's vivid recollection of its high arched windows, sinking headstones and moss-covered walls speaks to the heart of Irish storytelling where the lines between life and death, reality and fantasy, and salvation and damnation are hopelessly blurred. What happened or did not happen on that monastery wall just south of the chancel ---- brought her grandmother to tears more than eighty years later. **Spring 2017**

CPSIA information can be obtained at www.ICGtesting.com
Printed in the USA
BVOW05*1320170316

440704BV00002B/2/P